JUST WHEN STORIES

JUST WHEN STORIES

Beautiful
Books

www.beautiful-books.co.uk

Beautiful Books Limited
36-38 Glasshouse Street
London W1B 5DL

ISBN 9781905636204
9 8 7 6 5 4 3 2 1
First published 2010.

This anthology copyright © Beautiful Books Limited 2010; The Night of the Turtle Rescue copyright © Shaun Tan 2010; The Legend of Earthseasky copyright © Nury Vittachi 2010; Ladybirds for Lunch copyright © Hanif Kureishi 2010; The Schoolbag copyright © Kate Thompson 2010; Birds copyright © Radhika Jha 2010; Extract from The Wreck of the Zanzibar copyright © Michael Morpurgo 2010; The Morning After copyright © Polly Samson 2010; A Dream of Cranes copyright © Nirmal Ghosh; The Seahorse and the Reef copyright © Witi Ihimaera 2010; Camp K 101 copyright © William Boyd 2010; A Duck in India copyright © Alice Newitt 2010; Zushkaali and the Elephant copyright © Angela Young 2010; And the Dolphin Smiled copyright © Jin Pyn Lee 2010; George the Tortoise copyright © Antonia Michaelis 2010; Tiger, Tiger copyright © Lauren St John 2010; The Bear Who Wasn't There copyright © Raffaella Barker 2010; The River Nemunas copyright © Anthony Doerr, reprinted by permission of The Wendy Weil Agency, Inc; The Intrepid Dumpling's Dugong Story copyright © Louisa Young 2010; The Loris copyright © Romesh Gunesekera 2010.

Conceived, produced and edited by Tamara Gray.
Co-edited and co-produced by Amber Rust.

The right of the authors to be identified as the authors of this work have been asserted by them in accordance with the Copyright, Designs and Patents Act 1988.

All rights reserved. No part of this publication may be reproduced, stored in or introduced into a retrieval system, or transmitted, in any form, or by any means (electronic, mechanical, photocopying, recording or otherwise) without the prior written permission of the publisher. Any person who does any unauthorised act in relation to this publication may be liable to criminal prosecution and civil claims for damages. All efforts have been made to seek the approval of copyright owners to print material. Any omissions of which the publishers are informed will be rectified in future editions of the book.

A catalogue reference for this book is available from the British Library.

Cover design by Ian Pickard.
Illustrations by Maria Livings.
Typesetting by Misa Watanabe.

Printed and bound in the UK by CPI Mackays, Chatham ME5 8TD.

CONTENTS

Preface	1
The Night of the Turtle Rescue *by Shaun Tan*	9
The Legend of Earthseasky *by Nury Vittachi*	13
Ladybirds for Lunch *by Hanif Kureishi*	35
The Schoolbag *by Kate Thompson*	49
Birds *by Radhika Jha*	61
Extract from The Wreck of the Zanzibar *by Michael Morpurgo*	77
The Morning After *by Polly Samson*	93
A Dream of Cranes *by Nirmal Ghosh*	105
The Seahorse and the Reef *by Witi Ihimaera*	117

Camp K 101 *by William Boyd*	129
A Duck in India *by Alice Newitt*	149
Zushkaali and the Elephant *by Angela Young*	159
And the Dolphin Smiled *by Jin Pyn Lee*	179
George the Tortoise *by Antonia Michaelis*	187
Tiger, Tiger *by Lauren St John*	211
The Bear Who Wasn't There *by Raffaella Barker*	231
The River Nemunas *by Anthony Doerr*	239
The Intrepid Dumpling's Dugong Story *by Louisa Young*	283
The Loris *by Romesh Gunesekera*	295
Appendix	305

Preface
by Tamara Gray

Sincere thanks to those who have given me their support and encouragement and helped to make *Just When Stories* a reality: Simon at Beautiful Books for his belief; Sara and Ryan at Beautiful Books; Davy, David and Chris at Heavy Entertainment; Gui Altmayer at the Environmental Justice Foundation; Jonathon Harmsworth; George Thwaites; Fee Kennedy; Anna Phillips; Bob Benton and Steve Trent. Amber Rust who has been at my right hand over the last months.

Thanks to all the truly inspired children who entered the *Just When* Writing Competition whose work could make a wonderful book in itself.

So many thanks for writing *Just When Stories* go to William Boyd, Louisa Young, Romesh Gunesekera, Anthony Doerr, Nirmal Ghosh, Raffaella Barker, Witi Ihimaera, Radhika Jha, Hanif Kureishi, Antonia Michaelis, Michael Morpurgo, Jin Pyn Lee, Lauren St John, Shaun Tan, Kate Thompson, Nury Vittachi, Angela Young, Polly Samson and Alice Newitt.

Thank you to Romola Gerai, Eddie Redmayne, Hugh

Bonnerville, David Tennant and Martin Jarvis who have recorded stories for the *Just When* Audio CD and extra thanks to Hugh for making it happen. Everyone has donated their time, effort and work at no cost.

Thanks to Maria Livings for her stunning illustrations.

Thanks to you for buying this book. All profits will go to WildAid and the David Shepherd Wildlife Foundation, to support their work to stop the illegal wildlife trade.

The idea for *Just When Stories* came to me while reading *Just So Stories* by Rudyard Kipling to my children.

As my son delighted in the rhinoceros with itchy skin, I thought about the plight of the rhino today. When Kipling wrote his stories, rhino numbers stood at around 65,000. Today, less than 3,000 black rhinos survive.

Despite the fact that the trade in rhino horn has been banned for more than twenty years, demand for horn for use in traditional Chinese medicine remains strong.

Rhinos remain one of the most critically endangered species on the planet.

The rhinoceros, whale and leopard that feature at the heart of Kipling's *Just So Stories* now face imminent, permanent oblivion.

With *Just When Stories* I wanted to produce a book that

would raise awareness of these issues as well as being a collection of stories that would be fun and entertaining.

The title *Just When Stories* asks the questions: when will the irrational and cruel destruction of wildlife stop? And when will we take action to make it stop?

We need to answer that positively if today's generation of children are not to be the very last to have the chance to see, for example, a tiger in the wild.

Estimated at between $6 and $20 billion a year by Interpol, the illegal wildlife trade has drastically reduced numerous wildlife populations and currently has some teetering on the brink of extinction.

I have campaigned against the international illegal trade in endangered species since 1990. I think my energy comes from my mother Lana. During her short life, she campaigned passionately on behalf of women, despite the pressures of ill health. A love of animals comes perhaps from the lap of my grandfather, the British zoologist Sir James Gray, renowned for his work in animal locomotion and the development of experimental zoology. In particular Grandpa Gray is remembered for the Gray's Paradox on dolphin locomotion.

My early work as a photographer for the RSPCA led, at the age of 21, to a decision to dedicate myself to campaigning on behalf of animals. I have worked for some of the world's most effective and dynamic conservation organisations including The Environmental Investigation Agency (EIA), The David Shepherd Wildlife Foundation and WildAid. Within these organisations were and are some truly inspiring people, who I am honoured to have worked with over the years. People who work tirelessly, to undo the careless actions of a reckless world: Dave Currey, Allan Thornton, Pete Knights, Steve Trent, Rebecca Chen, Patrick Alley, Melanie Shepherd, David Shepherd, Steve Galster, Sue Fisher, Juliette Williams, Susie Watts, Dr Roz Reeve, Samantha Arditti, Debbie Banks amongst others, you ROCK.

As a mother of two children and a Trustee of WildAid, I wanted to make the book as appealing and accessible as possible. Each author has written a story in his or her own style and as such *Just When Stories* has become a family book. As the collection came together I realised that there would be a story for everyone.

My young daughter loves *The Intrepid Dumpling's Dugong Story*. Others I would suggest for younger readers are: *The Legend of Earthseasky*, *The Loris*, *The Bear Who Wasn't There*, *Ladybirds for Lunch*, *And The Dolphin Smiled*, *A Dream of Cranes* and *Zushkaali and the Elephant*.

For adults and teenagers I would guide you towards *The River Nemunas*, *Camp K 101*, *Tiger, Tiger*, *The Schoolbag*,

George the Tortoise, *The Seahorse and the Reef*, *A Duck in India*, *The Morning After* and *Birds*.

I hope that you enjoy reading these stories as much as I have enjoyed working with such wonderful writers to put them together. Please give a thought to the animals in this book. Perhaps you can learn something new and be inspired to take action. Together we can protect our endangered species for today's generation and the next.

My part in this book I dedicate to Elliot and Honor.
To my patient whippet Jake, more walks now I promise.

In aid of

The David Shepherd Wildlife Foundation

'Saving tigers, elephants, rhinos and other critically endangered mammals in the wild.'

DSWF is an adaptable and flexible, non-bureaucratic organisation responding promptly to conservation threats by supporting trusted, reputable individuals and organisations operating in the field.

Lean on administration but generous on funding, DSWF supports a range of innovative, vital and far-reaching projects throughout Africa and Asia, achieving real results for wildlife survival by:

- sending undercover agents into the field to investigate illegal wildlife crime;
- training and supplying anti-poaching patrols;
- establishing nature reserves and other protected areas;
- working with governments to establish conservation laws and regulations;
- educating wildlife consumers about the plight of the animals they 'use';
- teaching young people about endangered wildlife through art and school projects.

www.davidshepherd.org

Wildlife Foundation

WildAid

'When the buying stops the killing can too.'

WildAid's mission is to end the illegal wildlife trade within our lifetimes. To achieve this WildAid uniquely focuses on raising awareness to reduce the demand for threatened and endangered species products and to increase public support for wildlife conservation.

WildAid's successes have included:
- helping to secure international protection for the whale shark and basking shark under the UN's Convention on International Trade in Endangered Species (CITES);
- helping to secure shark finning bans in the US, EU, Costa Rica and Ecuador;
- helping to reduce consumption from 10 to 30% in Hong Kong, Taiwan, Thailand and Singapore;
- repeatedly reaching up to 1 billion viewers a week with celebrities asking consumers to stop purchasing illegal wildlife products.

www.wildaid.org

The Night of the Turtle Rescue

by Shaun Tan

The night of the turtle rescue, I thought we were going to die. I was clutching my hair and repeating the same questions over and over again: *Why do I always listen to your insane plans? Why aren't we at home watching TV like everyone else? What possible difference will any of this make?* I looked back and saw our pursuers relentlessly closing in, so much bigger and more powerful than we young fools with our pathetic ideals. *It's all over!* I yelled at the top of my voice. *Let's give ourselves up while we still have a chance!* And then, illuminated by the sweep of fierce searchlights, I saw our cargo for the first time: tiny limbs struggling to hold on, small unreadable faces staring out in all directions, voiceless mouths opening and closing. Nine small turtles—all we managed to save—just those nine. They turned their heads, looking back at me with eyes like black buttons, like full stops, blinking. I could think of only one thing, and it erupted from my lungs like a fireball as we hurtled into the darkness: *Keep going! Keep going! Keep going!*

The Legend of Earthseasky

by Nury Vittachi

Part one: The Legend of Earthseasky

The sun never rises on Earthseasky, the place where land, ocean and sky meet.

That's because it comes into existence only once a year, on the night when the great moontide sweeps the Eastern Oceans.

As the glowing moon reaches its zenith, tide-drawn waters rise all around what appears to be a deserted island containing nothing but dead trees and a long-sleeping volcano.

Seawater surges through undersea caves to find its way to the heart of the Isle of Nowhere, rising inside it to make a great lake in the bowl of the volcano.

At midnight on moontide, the ocean reaches the top of the volcano, salt-spray floating above the rim. The clouds bow down to form a ring around it.

And earth, sea and sky meet.

* * *

Part two: Silky Safaka and the Really Bad Idea

Since there is a place where earth, sea and sky meet, it

could also be a place where the inhabitants of earth, sea and sky meet. Sea creatures could meet land animals. Land animals could meet birds. Birds could meet fish.

That was the big idea of Silky Safaka, a rare white lemur who lived quietly by himself on a neighbouring island.

He thought his idea was an excellent one. For about two weeks.

Then he talked about it at length to a rather wise sea turtle and decided it was, in fact, a really bad idea.

The turtle had pointed out to him that some of the sea creatures would not want to just meet land animals; they would want to eat them. The land animals would want to eat the birds. And the birds would want to eat the fish.

But by the time this had become obvious, it was too late. He had already sent out the invitations. Whales had sung the invitation around the seven seas, birds had twittered it from the 12 skies, and land animals had barked and growled and howled it over countless mountains, forests and deserts.

The Summit of the Species was on.

* * *

Part three: Midnight on Moontide

At nightfall, darkness turned the ocean to a still pool of

the blackest ink.

But as the hours passed, rising moonlight sprinkled glitter on its surface. Night breezes chilled the air. Midnight-blooming trumpet-flowers scented it.

Moontide was coming.

Deep inside the Isle of Nowhere, stony veins and arteries gurgled as the salt waters rose. At the top of the mountain, a great lake started to form. Geysers gushed. Springs burst from the ground and trickled down the mountainsides. Clouds descended.

Silky Safaka sat in a large, dead tree on the lip of the volcano and waited for his guests to arrive. He wore a rectangular badge carrying the name of his species and the words: "Summit Organiser".

The lemur, a small, monkey-like creature with snow-white fur, a pinky-black face, and large, round eyes, looked up at the moon. It was nearly midnight.

The ocean, swirling blackly around the inside of the hollow volcano, belched as it crept higher and higher, sending fine sprays of mist to cool Silky's feet.

A small voice bubbled up from the water. 'I'm here. Am I the first?' said Angelshark.

'Yes,' said Silky, looking for Angelshark's badge and dropping it down to her. 'Here's your name tag.'

The lemur gave the small shark a welcoming smile, but inside he silently prayed that no one else would come.

Silky Safaka was only the size of a cat, and could easily be gobbled up by a peckish bird of prey, or a tiger or a crocodile. 'You're early. But I don't know if anyone else is coming. Maybe no one will.'

Angelshark laughed. 'Are you kidding? The message went all the way through the seven seas. EVERYONE is coming.'

A sudden flap of wings startled Silky Safaka. Black-Headed Coucal hovered in the sky.

'You scared me,' the lemur said.

'Better keep your wits about you,' cawed the bird. 'You do realize you've organized the most dangerous gathering in the history of the world?'

'It'll be fine,' said Silky, not believing a word he was saying. 'They'll all behave themselves.'

But he climbed a few branches higher in the tree, and looked behind him to identify escape routes.

Already, tiny undulating shadows had appeared in the distant sky and were starting to grow rapidly. Great flocks of birds were approaching.

At the same time, the water in the volcano lake started to seethe and boil as thousands of sea creatures found their way through the undersea caves to reach the surface of the volcano lake.

And the mountain itself quickly turned into a writhing, breathing thing, as thousands of land animals crept up its sides.

'Oh goodness me,' said Silky, gulping. 'It looks like everyone decided to come.'

* * *

Part four: The Problem of Snacks

The first meeting of all the creatures of the earth, sea and sky started every bit as badly as Silky had feared.

Most of the attendees were so transfixed by the sight of so much live food that they could do nothing but drool at each other. A steady drip-drip-drip of saliva drummed the rim of the lake and raised the water level.

In the lake, Great White Shark licked its lips so enthusiastically that it cut its tongue. As blood dripped into the water, the other sharks went wild. 'You cannibals,' the injured shark complained.

Overhead, Bald Eagle swooped around, circling particularly slowly over all the rodents. He refused to sit down.

Asiatic Lion kept asking: 'When are the snacks?' He made big eyes at the nervous Chinkara Gazelle next to him. She wanted to move but no one would change places with her.

As members found their badges, the various species of poultry, having decided that they were probably the favourite food group present, had an idea. They put up a large sign under Silky's tree saying: 'Isle of Nowhere is a Strictly Vegetarian Venue'.

The erection of this notice produced a chorus of groans, but it seemed to help everyone focus on the agenda. Silky Safaka wished he had prepared a table of healthy snacks somewhere away from the volcano rim.

He looked at the paper in front of him.

Item One: Declare meeting open.
Item two: Read minutes of previous meeting, if any.
Item three: Discuss stuff that needs to be discussed.

'Now, what would people like to discuss?' asked Silky. 'I've declared the meeting open, we have no previous minutes to read, and so we are already at item three.'

'Let's discuss food. When do we break for a snack?' asked Asiatic Lion.

'Never,' said Chinkara Gazelle. 'Never never never NEVER.'

'This is a VEGETARIAN venue,' clucked Red Junglefowl.

'There are no snacks,' Silky said. 'Members should exercise self-control and eat when they get home.'

A grumbly sort of silence descended. There was a general air of hostility and unhappiness.

Silky heard someone whisper to his neighbour: 'So why are we here?'

The black-faced white lemur decided that the only way to get a discussion going was to push it along himself. 'Now, to start with, let us identify what joint interests we all have,' he said.

'None,' said Asiatic Lion, tearing his hungry eyes away from Chinkara Gazelle, but only briefly. 'Except we all like eating each other. We all love fresh meat.'

'I prefer rotting meat,' said Griffon Vulture. 'It has more flavour.'

'No, fresh,' said Grey Wolf. 'It tastes fresher. That's logical.'

'Rotting meat has more protein,' said Nile Crocodile. 'All those worms and things, yum-yum.'

Silky put on his sternest face. 'May I remind you, this is a STRICTLY vegetarian event. Mental and verbal meat-eating are also banned. Please focus on the issue at hand. There must be something we have in common.'

Screech Owl tilted her head to one side, thinking. 'We all hate The Two-Legged Terror,' she said.

This produced much nodding among the members. 'Definitely,' agreed Arctic Seal.

'So, what do we do about it?' asked Silky.

There was another pause as the assembly considered this.

'Let's eat them,' roared Asiatic Lion.

'YES,' agreed many of those present. Drool flowed like streams.

'No MEAT-EATING,' said Domestic Chicken. 'No meat-eating of any kind may be discussed, planned or thought about.'

Silky picked up a gavel he had made from a twig and a nut and banged the hollow tree trunk below him for silence. 'Quiet please, I need a sensible proposal.'

'I propose we break for supper,' said Asiatic Lion, licking his neighbour.

There was a roar of agreement from the would-be diners and a chorus of nervous shrieks from the prospective dinners.

Silky sighed. He looked from face to face around him, in the water below, and in the sky above. In all directions he saw suspicion, mistrust and fear, and above all, hunger.

He decided to close the meeting as soon as possible. Black-Headed Coucal had been right. This was the most dangerous gathering on earth.

'If no one has anything constructive to suggest, I suggest we move on to item four, which is to declare the meeting closed,' he said, glancing behind to make sure his escape route was still clear. 'Let us treat this as an initial meet-and-greet event, with follow-up gatherings to be arranged if generally considered worthwhile.'

But when he turned his head back to the crowd, he noticed that a small furry creature had raised its hand.

* * *

Part five: The Question of the Potoroo

'You have an issue to raise?' Silky Safaka asked.

'Yes. I am a Potoroo,' said the creature. 'I am known as Gilbert's Potoroo, to be precise. I have a question.' He paused. For a long time. He dropped his eyes to his feet and looked rather embarrassed.

Silky, impatient, decided to prompt him. 'Which is?'

Gilbert's Potoroo cleared his throat before replying. 'It is a very important question, and it is this: just when am I going to get a girlfriend?'

Asiatic Lion roared with laughter and the other mammals joined in, anxious to keep on good terms with him. 'This is not a dating club, Gilbert,' he said.

Gilbert's Potoroo raised himself to his full height, which was about the size of a rabbit. 'This is not a matter of dating. This is a matter of the utmost importance. It is a matter of avoiding *Extinction*.'

There was instant silence.

Someone had said the *E* word.

It was as if a bright light had been switched on in a dark room.

'Thanks to the Two-Legged Terror, I am the last of my kind,' the Potoroo said.

It was so quiet that the single drip of drool that someone let fall sounded like a pounding hammer.

In the quietness, a small shark popped its head up from the very back of the lake. 'Just when am I going to find a boyfriend?' she said. 'I am Dumb Gulper Shark from Taiwan and I think I may also be the last of my species.'

Next to her, Baiji Dolphin popped her head out of the water. 'Just when will I have children?' she asked. 'I am also the last of my kind.'

From a moss-covered rock under Silky's tree, a lizard-like creature waved its tail to get attention. 'Just when will I find a partner? Blue Iguanas like me are almost Extinct.'

'I'm Extinct too, nearly,' said Northern Hairy-Nosed Wombat.

'And me,' said a monkey whose name-tag identified him as Miss Waldron's Red Colobus.

'And me,' said a sad, frowning bird wearing a nametag which said Blue-Crowned Laughing Thrush.

'Just when will I find love?' asked De Winton's Golden Mole. 'I am all alone.'

'Just when will I get someone to fertilize my eggs?' said

Gorgeted Puffleg. 'Otherwise my kind will disappear.'

Suddenly everyone was talking at once.

Silky hammered with his gavel. 'Silence, please. One at a time, please,' he squealed. He had no idea how to respond. He turned to look at Gilbert's Potoroo. 'I'm not really sure how we can help you or anyone else. This is a problem that many of us face, including me.'

A kangaroo was jumping up and down to get Silky's attention. 'Mr Summit Organiser, Mr Summit Organiser,' he said.

'Sit down please, Kangaroo,' said Silky. 'There are lots of you around, Kangaroo, sir. You're definitely not extinct.'

'True, but I have important news for Gilbert's Potoroo,' he said. 'I saw a lonely potoroo just like him down in Two Peoples Bay in Western Australia. I can take him down there after the meeting if he wants.'

'Was she cute?' asked Gilbert's Potoroo.

'As a button,' said Kangaroo.

'Can we leave right now?'

Silky was surprised and delighted at this turn of events. At last something worthwhile had been achieved. To save a species from Extinction was a big thing. 'Well, that's very helpful, thank you very much. Anybody else have any problem-solving suggestions?'

'I saw a Baiji dolphin in the far western reaches of the

Yangtze river in China,' said Bald Eagle, finally settling down on a branch. 'I still remember the spot and I will be happy to show our friend where it is.'

A Jellyhead Octopus waved seven of his eight legs from the lake to get the meeting's attention. 'A small colony of dumb gulper sharks was recently found off Flinders Island, Tasmania,' she said. 'You're not the last one, my friend.'

Excited chattering broke out across the gathering. Silky banged his gavel as loud as he could, but nobody stopped talking. All the arrivals were swapping notes on the species that lived near them.

'One at a time, please,' said Silky.

The lemur used his monkey-like limbs to clamber swiftly up the tree to the branches near the top, where he found one which appeared to balance the structure. He rapidly jumped up and down on it until the entire tree was shaking.

He was in charge of this meeting and he was NOT going to lose control. 'Silence, please,' he shrieked. 'Silence!'

Giant Panda jumped up and grabbed one of the branches. 'Let me help,' she said. 'I can shake the tree harder than you.'

She pulled down with all her weight, bending the tree almost in half.

'Now let go,' said Silky.

Panda did as she was told. The tree whipped back upright, and Silky shot high into the air.

Numerous hungry mouths opened below him, following his trajectory.

Food was back on the agenda.

* * *

Part six: The Species Find a Mission

The white lemur landed in the water with a giant splash.

The Great White Shark shot like a torpedo in his direction, licking his lips again.

'Stop! This is a strictly veg—' said Silky.

But he couldn't finish his sentence. A tentacle whipped around his waist and punched the air out of him. He was yanked up and out of the water by Colossal Squid, who held him high in the air, out of reach of the snapping shark.

Then Bald Eagle swooped out of the brightening sky and plucked the lemur out of the squid's grip.

'Wait! Where are you taking me?' Silky screamed.

The great bird languidly flapped his huge wings and took him back to his tree. He sat on his branch, stunned, and shook himself.

The drama of his journey to and from his tree placed

The Legend of Earthseasky

the lemur back at the centre of attention.

'Ladies and gentlemen,' Silky puffed, his heart beating as if it would burst. 'We have a purpose. We have an objective. We have an aim. We have a mission. The issue is Extinction. The enemy is the Two-Legged Terror. Almost every species on earth is suffering individually. But if we work together, we can help each other. We can beat the threat of Extinction.'

Every creature present cheered at this. Even the animals who could not hear anything that Silky had said (after all, some didn't have ears) thought it a good idea to join in the general triumphant hollering. A hooting and a howling and a clapping and a hissing and a squeaking and a chirping and a barking and a roaring filled the night air as never before. The cacophony floated out across the ocean.

Silky, now that he had the ear of the attendees again, turned out to be a natural crowd controller.

He let the cheering continue for a good three minutes, and then, just as the racket was dying down, he climbed to the very highest, thinnest branch of the dead tree. His weight made the tree lean over towards the middle of the lake, putting him right at the centre of attention.

'We MUST work together,' he pleaded. 'The Two-Legged Terror is a dangerous enemy with powerful weapons intent on destroying species and the planet, even though it will wipe itself out along with the rest of us.'

Yellow-Tailed Woolly Monkey waved her bright tail. 'I have some inside information that can help us, I'm sure. It is SECRET data that can help us fight the Two-Legged Terror.'

At the word "secret", everyone turned to stare at the monkey.

Agile and thin-limbed, she used Hippo and several sea-creatures as stepping stones to cross the lake. She quickly scampered up the tree and sat next to Silky.

'My cousins who live in a forest near a city have been studying the Two-Legged Terror for years. The evil creatures have been destroying us and our homes for as long as anyone can remember. But they have recently been infiltrated by people sympathetic to us.'

Asiatic Lion whispered to Chinkara Gazelle: 'What is she saying?'

'Enemies have sneaked into their midst,' Chinkara Gazelle replied.

The monkey continued: 'A small group of creatures has quietly moved into the homes of the Two-Legged Terrors. They look similar to the Terrors, except they are smaller, cuter, and smarter. But more importantly, they love animals. They love birds. They love fish. My cousins have seen them being openly and luxuriantly affectionate to the whole spectrum of creatures, from tiny hamsters to huge horses.'

Silky was amazed. 'What is this creature called?'

Yellow-Tailed Woolly Monkey wrinkled her brow: 'They are called chilblains, or something like that.'

Bottle-Nosed Dolphin leapt out of the lake and spoke in mid-air. 'The word is not chilblain. It is children,' she said. 'What the monkey says is true. They are small and clever and they are on our side. They are our best hope.'

* * *

Part seven: A Future

The moon fell. The dark grey sky was tinted navy blue and slivers of pink appeared on the horizon. It was time for the first Summit of the Species to come to an end.

Silky Safaka was elected general-director of the organization. A committee was set up to work on ways to co-operate secretly with the small two-legged infiltrators to halt the mass Extinction that was taking place.

Dawn rose slowly over the Isle of Nowhere as the great moontide retreated. The lake bubbled and began to vanish for another year. Thousands of living creatures started to make their way homewards.

Silky sat in his tree, stunned and exhausted by the drama of the night.

Then he heard something inside the volcano: a voice. It sounded as if his name was being called.

The lemur carefully climbed out onto that thinnest of branches. The tree leaned into the hole where the lake had been. He looked down.

The lake had retreated at high speed and was now far, far down, deep inside the dark, empty heart of the volcano. In the water, he could see the head of Great White Shark. His mouth was moving. He was saying something.

'I can't hear you,' Silky shouted.

The shark continued to talk. He seemed animated and excited, surging around the lake. Clearly he had what he considered an important message to deliver.

'I can't hear you,' Silky repeated. 'Tell me next time.'

The branch cracked. It and its passenger fell.

'Oops,' said the lemur.

Silky fell into the darkness of the volcano, heading straight for the shark's mouth. Down, down, down, he fell—a journey which seemed to take ages.

He landed in the water with a tremendous splash that knocked every particle of air out of his small lungs.

He went deep down into the cold blackness before

he managed to get his bearings and swim back up to the surface.

Treading water and gasping for breath, he saw the Great White Shark bearing down on him at high speed, his mouth open.

'Help, help,' the lemur shouted.

The shark smiled with a thousand teeth.

'Help, help,' screamed the lemur.

'I have something to show you,' the shark said. 'Hold your breath and grab hold of my dorsal fin.'

Silky clambered onto the shark's back and snatched a breath before he was dunked back underwater.

He felt himself being whisked through a series of underwater caves, and then up and out into the ocean surrounding the island.

The shark took him right out into the open sea. Silky wondered whether he was being taken to the shark's home territory—or perhaps the shark had decided to give him a free ride to his own home. But no, the shark went right past the lemur's home island.

After a journey of two hours at high speed, another island came into view: a large, green land with tall, odd-shaped trees which looked like upside-down umbrellas.

The shark skidded into the shallow water on a white, floury beach.

'You can get off now,' he said. 'This is where I wanted to take you.'

'Thank you,' said the lemur, jumping onto the sand. 'Where am I?'

The shark smiled. 'I've taken you to an island which you may not have visited before. There's a very rare creature living on it. A Silky Safaka. A female one.'

Silky was speechless. Great White Shark turned and headed back out to the open sea, under a wide morning sky that was now pink and blue.

Silky Safaka started to walk inland, his amazed eyes scanning the trees.

Ladybirds for Lunch

by Hanif Kureishi

It was a special occasion, a party day.

The identical twins Theo and Jake knew it was, because immediately after breakfast their mother scrubbed the remains of all baked beans, bits of egg, and pieces of toast from their hair. Then, as she hurriedly fitted them into their matching Chinese silk jackets, the boys noticed another strange sight. Their father was helping in the kitchen. It was most unusual for him to wander that far from the television, particularly in the morning.

The two boys looked out of the window and saw what a lovely day it was going to be for a lunch party in the garden. Rather unusually, the sun was shining and the few flowers the boys hadn't flattened with their football seemed to be glowing in the misty morning air.

This wasn't just any old lunch, said father, crouching down and adopting his "listen-to-me-seriously" voice. Unfortunately though, since he had decided to let his sideburns grow and now looked as though two hairy slugs had settled on the side of his face, Theo and Jake found it difficult not to giggle when he was talking, and had to keep pinching one another.

All the same, they were informed by their father's pointing finger that the guests, Frazer and Sabina Binswanger, were very important people who helped decide on the programmes that appeared on television. And since mother hadn't had a job for over a year, she was very keen to have Mr Binswanger employ her.

Father added that the Binswangers had a villa in France with a swimming pool and servants, where the most glamorous and exciting people went to escape London and meet everyone they knew. Mother and Father desperately wanted to be invited to this fashionable gathering. Except, there was one problem. The Binswangers only liked children some of the time, and not all of the time. If the family were to receive an invitation the boys had to be on their best behaviour today, and must allow themselves to be kissed, tickled, tousled and tossed in the air, when required, by the Binswangers.

'Best behaviour,' promised Theo.

'We are the good boys!' said Jake.

They slapped hands with their father and each other, and skipped out into the garden.

Excitement mounted all morning. Father frantically searched the house for an item of clothing unstained by crushed biscuit. Mother hunted for her curlers. This involved her glaring at the probable culprits Jake and Theo: she had to "enter the mind of the criminal" before foraging in the obvious places. One curler was in the fridge, embedded in the butter, another was installed in the front of the video recorder, and the last one had been neatly placed in the watering can.

Then, with her curlers in—and her head looked like a bowl of pasta—mother went into the garden with a trowel to shovel up the numerous piles of cat poo. Cats came from miles around, she claimed, to crap exclusively on her earth. Glancing furtively around to ensure that no one from the Neighbourhood Watch was looking—she was a leading member—mother hurled the cat droppings over the fence into the next garden and scurried back into the house.

The cats were practically the only wildlife there was in Shepherd's Bush, apart from the people on the street, and of course the beautiful ladybirds, hundreds of which congregated around the garden bench to compare spots and talk about what was happening.

While mother and father rushed in and out of the house carrying bread and wine, cutlery and napkins, and laying them on a trestle table covered with a white tablecloth, Jake and Theo, playing in a corner of the garden, had gone very quiet. On a normal day such a silence would have aroused suspicion. But today their parents were too busy to notice.

Theo had gathered a group of ladybirds in his hand and was intending to place them, for the afternoon, in a cardboard box, so the insects could party together. Jake was hunting for others in order to give them to Theo. Once the ladybirds were gathered in the concert hall of the box, the boys—who loved to play mad jigs on their numerous instruments—would make music and watch them dance.

Before the boys had located a box, they were disturbed by voices.

Frazer and Sabina Binswanger, the important guests with important names, were entering the garden like Royalty at a film premier. Sabina's jewellery jingle-jangled and her high heels punctured Father's new lawn, while Frazer's confident voice boomed across the neighbourhood. They both wore sharp perfumes, which caused all flies in the vicinity to immediately become unconscious. However, the ladybirds—snug in the warm booth of Jake and Theo's hands—were not affected.

The boys tried to disappear under a hedge but mother was calling for them to greet the Binswangers. Theo quickly looked around for somewhere to lodge his insect friends until after lunch. But there was nowhere—until he spied a crusty pie with a hole in the top, sitting conveniently on the table. He thrust the ladybirds into the pie.

'Good idea,' said Jake, doing the same thing.

Theo hastily covered over the gap with a loose piece of pastry, and they pushed each other towards the outstretched arms of the guests.

They all sat down to lunch.

The cutlery clinked, wine was poured and the voices rose. Theo and Jake, who had Sabina's lipstick kisses imprinted on their cheeks and forehead like pink butterflies, smiled up politely at the Binswangers as instructed. Occasionally either Frazer or Sabina would grab the end of one or other boy's nose, as if they were public property, and give them a sudden hard twist. This was their way of being friendly, which the boys knew they had to bear if they were to be invited to France on holiday.

Meanwhile the boys were kicking one another under the table. They knew they had to do something about the ladybirds, who were suffocating inside the pie. Theo whispered to Jake that they had to try and release them.

But as Theo leant over to grab the pie, his mother tapped him on the wrist:

'Wait a minute,' she scolded. 'Guests first!'

'But mum—'

How could he explain?

'Mum!' echoed Jake, as she cut into it.

It was too late. A moment later a piece of the pie was on Frazer Binswanger's plate.

'Yum, yum,' he said, licking his lips. 'I'm very hungry.' He looked at mother. 'Everyone says your food is wonderful.'

Ladybirds for Lunch

'Thank you,' she said, with a happy smile, thinking of her new job.

Soon the pie would be in Mr Binswanger's mouth. Theo and Jake could only look on in dismay.

Now Frazer Binswanger was a man of such sophistication and importance that he was allowed to have bad manners. Theo and Jake watched as he picked up the pie with both hands, put it to his mouth and took such a large bite that they thought he might swallow the whole world.

'This is delicious,' he said, spitting out bits of pastry, one of which struck Jake above the eye.

Jake removed the pastry from his eyebrow and looked at Theo. They knew ladybirds were rather crunchy but soft inside, like tiny prawns. With sauce they might be tasty: but it was not a good idea to eat them alive, particularly if you were unprepared for the experience.

'Delicious!' said Frazer Binswanger.

As Mr Binswanger's teeth champed into the crust again, the ladybirds hurried out of the pie, rushing away like dodgem cars propelled by silent electricity. Some of them flew into the air, but many others, drawn by the heat of Mr Binswanger's face, merely crawled over his soft, sticky cheeks and settled down in a swoon, having swallowed the alcohol he was sweating. Others ran about in a panic, not knowing where they were.

Jake and Theo saw their father notice this first. His eyes widened and he glanced fearfully at mother. Looking at Frazer Binswanger's face she almost fell backwards off her chair in horror. She would never work again!

Then Sabina Binswanger, with her fork at her mouth, glanced up to see a whole company of ladybirds moving across her husband's face.

Mr Binswanger so loved to talk that he failed to realise the pink surface of his face was spotted with moving dots. In fact, several were already swinging from the dark hairs that stuck out of the top of his nose like wires (it was said they could pick up foreign TV and radio stations, like aerials). Everyone watched in fascination as one of these ladybirds then trotted up his nostril like an explorer in the rain forest. Other ladybirds lined up to run into the mysterious and winding caverns of his ears, clambering over bits of old potato and carrot lodged there, until a battalion of them entered the spacious living room of his mind.

Jake looked at Sabina Binswanger in amazement. She had stuffed her napkin into her mouth. Theo wondered if she was so hungry that she wanted to eat it. But he realised she was trying to stop herself laughing.

When Mr Binswanger saw the astonished faces of his friends around the table and felt what was happening to him, his red face turned the colour of a peeled potato.

Soon he was aware that the living room of his mind was alive with ladybirds. He threw down his knife and fork, pushed away his plate and began to knock himself on the side of the head with his fist. He began to wave around in his chair like a tree in a strong wind.

'Something not nice has happened to me!' he moaned in disbelief. 'I've been invaded by aliens!'

It was true. Theo and Jake knew ladybirds loved parties and that by now they would be making themselves comfortable inside Mr Binswanger's mind. Soon they might be swinging from the light fittings, playing records and videos, smoking cigarettes and even dancing.

But it was also obvious to the twins that banging yourself above the ear, was no way to extract insects from inside your head. The thudding noise would only frighten the ladybirds and they would scuttle deeper and deeper into the interior, perhaps into the memory area, so that every dream of the past that Bingswanger now had, would be sprinkled with ladybirds, like pepper on an omelette.

What could the boys do? It was an emergency.

Usually their mother rid the garden of ants by pouring boiling water over them. But the twins knew their chances of going on holiday to France wouldn't improve if they shot hot water up Frazer Binswanger's nose or into his ears.

Without saying anything, the same thought occurred to the boys simultaneously.

Theo threw back his chair and dashed into the house to fetch his tambourine and a pan and spoon. Jake jumped up and raced indoors for his battery-operated keyboard. They sprinted out into the garden and began to play a cool bossa nova. They had rehearsed this song many times. It was one of their favourites. But still Jake and Theo were nervous. Mother and father were glaring at them with very serious 'I'll-get-you-for-this-later' looks on their faces.

Theo and Jake knew that all insects, like all children, could be moved by music. The boys' sweet voices rose like doves into the air, and across West London the ears of shoppers pricked up. People dropped their bags to feel the delicious rhythm working through them.

As the music swung, even Sabina Binswanger's foot bounced and she clapped her hands. But Mr Binswanger, who had gone rigid with distress and annoyance, remained perfectly still as the ladybirds frolicked on the levers and wheels of his mind.

After a few moments everyone saw, pushing through the opening of one of his hairy nostrils, the black and white head of a ladybird. But they could also see that Mr Binswanger, with a cruel and vengeful expression on his face, was about to crush it into jam between his

Ladybirds for Lunch

thumb and finger.

Jake shook his head wildly and Theo banged furiously on the pan. Squashing a ladybird wouldn't encourage the others to come out. Surely Frazer Binswanger understood that? Adults could be very stupid at times.

Fortunately, heeding Jake and Theo's warning, Mr Binswanger refrained from his murderous action. And as the rhythm of the music built, the ladybirds began to emerge from his ears and nose into the sunshine, shaking their bottoms and waving their legs. Some of them looked a little dazed, as anyone would, had they spent time within the foggy labyrinth of Mr Binswanger's brain. But most were dancing, and many gathered on Mr Binswanger's forehead, where they hopped and capered like a line of animated billiard balls.

Soon they were all out and Mr Binswanger's face returned to its natural Ribena colour. Once more Sabrina was laughing and drinking. Mother and father were so relieved they even smiled at one another. The boys, settled under the table, played a calm Moroccan tune that they were perfecting.

'Those boys can certainly play,' said Sabrina, clicking her fingers and resisting her desire to twist their noses.

'But they are often quiet too,' father explained firmly. 'Sometimes for hours... and hours... and hours on end.'

'Yes!' confirmed mother.

'Not too quiet, I hope,' said Sabrina. 'For they'll certainly entertain the other guests on holiday in France—if they bring their instruments!'

'But we're always telling them to shut up,' said mother.

'I wouldn't do that,' said Sabrina. 'Those boys have talent!'

'Talent!' murmured Frazer. He lit a big cigar and relaxed after his disturbing experience. Talent was his favourite word. He loved to say it, but most of all he loved to find it, particularly in his own neighbourhood, and during lunch. 'I'm going to put those boys on a television show. They really helped me out. Those ladybirds were tickling my brain so much I thought I'd go insane!'

'I wonder, though,' murmured Sabina, 'How they got in that pie in the first place?'

'I don't know,' said father, looking uneasily at the innocent faces of his identical sons, 'But people say that ladybirds always follow the talent!'

'Like me,' said Frazer Binswanger, sipping his drink, and patting the boys on the head. 'Jake and Theo—play on please!'

And they picked up their instruments and sang.

The Schoolbag

by Kate Thompson

Where the dust road crossed the creek, the boy stopped. The brindle shade of the redgums often tricked him there, but this time there really was something unusual among the rock-rubble of the empty river bed. A large animal was sitting there, watching him.

He dropped his schoolbag at his feet. It made the wrong sort of noise as it hit the ground, but only a small and ignored part of his mind noticed this. Most of his attention was taken by the animal. It was so still and so silent, and it blended so well into the shadows that he had difficulty in making out exactly what it was.

'Hello,' said the boy.

The animal opened its mouth twice, but no sound came out. Its eyes were soft and brown. It was a dog, surely.

'Where did you come from?' the boy said. There were no dogs in the area apart from his own one, which never strayed far from the house. There were no other houses for a wandering dog to come from. It was fifteen kilometres to the next station, and twenty to the town.

A yellow tailed black cockatoo soared in from the bush beyond the creek and settled on a high branch. The dog stood, and as it did so he saw that it wasn't like any dog he had ever seen. Its tail was too long and too fat. Its hind legs were the wrong shape. He was intrigued,

The Schoolbag

and he was afraid it was getting up to leave, disturbed by the arrival of the cockatoo. But when it moved, it came towards him, padding softly on massive paws.

The boy took a step backwards. His foot hit the bag, which made the wrong noise again. Books don't rattle. But then, why would he be carrying books? He could hardly remember the last time the school bus had come to bring him into town. What had made him think he would be carrying books?

Stripes. The dog that wasn't a dog had stripes across its back. He had seen that before. There was a picture of it in his mind. He knew he ought to remember what it was, but he didn't. And it was still padding towards him. He lifted the bag by its shoulder strap, ready to swing. It was the only weapon he had, but it was too light to be of any use.

And in any case, he didn't need it. The dog thing stopped at the edge of the road and sat down again, quite calm and not remotely threatening. They were both in full sunlight now. The heat was intense, but the boy noticed with pleasure that it wasn't bothering him at all. His father was like that. He would work all day in the fields, winter or summer, hardy and rugged as a lizard. It was his mother who fussed about sunnies and hats and sunblock. He was surprised she had let him out of the house at all, with the sun so high and strong.

He held out a hand to the animal and rubbed his fingertips together. 'Here boy. Here, funny dog.'

'Not a dog,' the animal said.

'No?' said the boy. 'What are you, then? A wolf?'

'Did you ever see a wolf with stripes?' said the dog-wolf thing, twisting slightly to give the boy a better view of its back.

'No,' said the boy. 'Tigers have stripes. Are you a tiger?'

The dogwolftiger thing gave a humorous snort and sat up on its hind legs. It put a broad paw on its midriff. 'Did you ever see a tiger with a pouch?'

'No,' said the boy. There were no baby dogwolftiger things in there, but it was definitely a pouch, just like the roos and wallabies had. That picture was in his thoughts again. A photograph somewhere. But the knowledge of what this creature was had got locked away in the depths of his mind, along with the memory of what he was carrying in the bag, and of where he was coming from and going to. And since he ought to know, it seemed to him that it would have been bad manners to ask the animal what its name was. Instead he said, 'So tell me this. What are you doing here?'

'I'm returning,' said the dogwolftigerroo. 'Just like you.'

A green rosella and a brilliant blue wren joined the cockatoo in the gum tree. They all sat on the same branch, looking down like the audience at a theatre.

The Schoolbag

'Returning?' said the boy.

The dogwolftigerroo stood up and stretched itself, then opened its long jaws impossibly wide. Its teeth were formidable, but somehow the boy knew that this behaviour was not threatening; something more along the lines of a limbering-up exercise. When it had once again settled itself on its powerful haunches, the dogwolftigerroo began its story.

'I used to live here,' it said. 'I lived here for a long, long, long time. I had no friends because I was inclined to eat anything that came close enough to talk to, but I had no enemies either, because I was the biggest beast in the bush and had by far the most dangerous bite. There were good years and bad years, but on the whole this was a fine place to live and hunt and bring up my children.'

The boy loved stories, and he wanted to sit down so he could relax while he listened. A schoolbag full of books would have made a comfortable seat, but just in time he remembered the rattle, so he sat down on the road instead.

'Then the blackfella came,' the dogwolftigerroo went on. 'He gave me a fright, that blackfella did, with his fires and his spears and his sneaking about in the bush. He became my enemy; my first one. I had to learn a whole new set of tricks to keep out of his way and the way of his fires and his spears. I did learn them and I stayed out of his reach. Once I got used to the new ways, I had to admit that this was still a pretty good place to live and hunt and bring up my children. And so it continued to be for a long, long, long time.'

The boy stretched himself full length on the road beneath the white glare of the sun. His mother would complain about the dust on his shirt. Not enough water for washing any more. But he never got as dusty and dirty as his father did, out on the land. When he thought of his father, a blink of a memory returned to him. The growling and complaining of heavy machinery. That was all.

'Anyway,' the dogwolftigerroo was saying, 'as it turned out, the blackfella was a friend compared to what came next.' It stopped and gazed, with a melancholy expression, into the middle distance.

'What?' said the boy. 'What did come next?'

'Mmm,' said the dogwolftigerroo. 'Sheep. What came next was sheep.' It fell silent, musing, and a brief image visited the boy. Dirty heaps of something, scattered everywhere across the farm. It was connected to what his father was doing, the machines, the dust. While he waited for the story to continue, he rested his cheek on his elbow and looked up into the gum tree. A pair of possums had draped themselves comfortably there, long tails dangling. From the unseen bush beyond he

The Schoolbag

could hear the glassy warbling of a magpie, and for some reason the sound unsettled him. It was as familiar to him as the sound of his own breath, but he hadn't heard it for ages, and there was a reason for that. He just couldn't remember what it was.

The dogwolftigerroo took up the story again, and the boy was glad, because he wasn't at all sure he wanted to pursue those particular thoughts any further.

'The thing about sheep,' it said, 'is that they're not very smart. There are a lot of good things about sheep. They are very slow and very tasty. And, compared to most of the edible things in this land, they are very large. But they are not strong on ideas, or the execution of them. If it had been left to the sheep, there would have been no problem. They wouldn't have been any threat to me at all.

'But it wasn't left to them. It wasn't the sheep that came up with this 'either them or me' idea. It was the whitefella. And it was the whitefella who carried it out, right to the bitter end.'

The magpie had stopped singing, but the boy's sense of unease was still there. Sheep. Those dirty heaps in the dust. Fleeces torn and flapping.

'It wasn't enough for the whitefella to take a share from the forests like the blackfella did,' said the dogwolftigerroo. 'No. He had to cut them down and burn them, and make fields for his millions of fat, delicious sheep. And he had no intention of sharing anything with anyone, least of all with me.'

The magpie flew low over the boy's head and swooped up into the gum tree. It shouldn't be there. It couldn't be there.

'I ran and I raced and I sped and I slunk and I fled and I crouched and I crept and I hid and I went far, far into the deepest depths and creeks and hollows and shadows and dens. But there was nowhere in the length and breadth of my world where the whitefella wouldn't follow. He trapped me and put me in a cage and sent me across the sea. He killed me for sport and he killed me for money and he killed me for glory. He killed me when it was lawful and he killed me when it was unlawful. He killed me until he couldn't kill me any more, because I wasn't there for him to kill. He had wiped me out entirely.'

The boy was still looking into the tree. It wasn't only the magpie that shouldn't be there. None of those creatures should be there. The tree itself shouldn't be there. It couldn't be. It had dropped those branches, one by one, in a useless attempt to save itself from the drought that didn't end. The drought that killed the sheep and had his father digging huge holes with the backhoe to bury them in, while all around him, and all across the whole country, the birds dropped dead and dying from the sky.

The Schoolbag

The pain of remembering hit him. He stood up and picked up his bag. But it was too late now to run away from the memories. Another one surged in, of that final morning, when there was no one left except for him, and the sun rose above the stripped and silent land and showed him its white-hot teeth.

'So you're like me,' he said, at last remembering the name of the dogwolftigerroo. 'You're the only one left. The very last of the Tasmanian tigers?'

The thylacine shook its long, heavy head. 'I am not the last,' it said. 'I have already told you. I am returning, like this tree and all the creatures in it. We are all of us extinct, now. Even you, with your little bag of bones, there. Why don't you sit down again, and tell us all your story?'

Birds

by Radhika Jha

When I moved to Mumbai from Lucknow I knew that most of all, I'd miss the birds. So, on that last morning, I woke early, made myself a cup of tea and took it out into the garden. I was all alone. The garden was like a dark cave. It was too cold for the birds to show themselves yet, but I knew they were there, watching me from the comfort of their nests. When I looked back at the house I knew I would not miss it, or the people that lived in it: parents, grandparents, uncles, aunts, decrepit and smelly dogs and nosy servants.

So I said goodbye. To the faithful Hornbills, the worried looking green barbet, the red vented bulbuls, the glossy koyals, the peacocks and mynas. Goodbye bald headed vultures, goodbye golden backed woodpecker— I'm off to the big city.

As a child I would dream of becoming a bird. Not because they could fly and I couldn't. But because of their colours. Who ever thought of putting grey with copper, black with orange. Purple with green and russet. When I tried to wear the same combinations in my clothes they never looked quite right. Even as an adult, every time I saw a new species of bird, I felt the same mix of awe and envy.

When I arrived in Mumbai, I stayed in the empty

Birds

apartment of a family friend in Colaba. Pigeons shat on the pavement from the trees on my street. I would watch them as I drank my tea in the morning and wonder disdainfully if they were the only kinds of birds to be found in Mumbai. After a few days not speaking to anyone, I realized that the pigeons weren't so boring after all. Their sensible grey overcoats were actually liberally splashed with a dull mother of pearl purple with shiny copper overtones and an iridescent grey-green. Meanwhile, I was forced to go further and further north in my search for a reasonable rent. Each day I took the train through miles of evil smelling concrete with hardly a tree to be seen anywhere. What trees I saw looked foreign, like refugees or illegal immigrants, timidly hiding between the buildings. And then there was the smell of the city. Sewage and sea. It was everywhere—and only served to compound my loneliness.

In the end I decided upon Bandra, a once beautiful northern suburb. Like everywhere in Mumbai, Bandra had lots of buildings. Built over the carcasses of old red tiled houses, these newly built apartment blocks poked their scrawny necks out of a sea of emerald rainforest. Trees were to buildings what birds were to me. The latter looked fat, blockish and unimaginative, lacking the architectural grace and complication of even the most ordinary tree. But Mumbai seemed to like these contrasts.

The apartment I moved into was on the fourth floor. But since it was built into the side of a hill, I was lucky enough to be able to see trees on the left hand corner. Directly in front stood the ugly peeling façade of another building whose tinted windows looked like a blind man's glasses. One flat in particular, the one a floor higher than mine, attracted my attention because it was so expensively furnished. The windows of the flat were the only ones that weren't tinted and the inside of the flat looked very modern and minimalist, like something you might see in the pages of an interior design magazine. Only the bedroom remained hidden, muffled in heavy silk curtains.

My apartment in contrast was nothing more than a single large room divided in the middle. One side was bedroom and the other living room. There was no balcony but giant windows made up one entire wall. Because my work was done on the computer, the window quickly became my most important contact with the world.

Easily the most impressive tree in the compound was a venerable old banyan, almost five storeys high, and at least two hundred years old I guessed. My window looked directly into its biggest branches, and if I leaned over a little I could look down to where the tree began just above the far left corner wall of my building's compound. Someone had built a shrine at the base of the tree and red and yellow thread was wrapped around the trunk. But what really interested me was not what humans had done to the tree but what the birds had done to it. For the tree was like an apartment building. At each level, it was inhabited by a different species of bird. On the top were the birds of prey—hawks and falcons mostly, though sometimes an eagle would arrive for a short while, frightening the others away. Right beside them, tolerated and ignored by the big birds, were a group of twenty or so very busy little birds whose name I never discovered. They were pale grey and black with red throats and red under the wings. I adored them and a glimpse of their happy red was enough to fill me with delight all day.

The middle branches, those that were directly in front of my flat were populated almost entirely by crows and a few pigeons. There were so many of them and they looked at me in such a knowing way when I sat at my window that I felt sure that one day they would attack and the glass would prove to be a useless defense against their razor sharp beaks. But they never did, preferring to fight and argue endlessly amongst themselves. There were two groups who sat facing each other on separate branches, the left hand group sat on branches that were slightly higher than the right hand group. Like the Montagues and the Capulets, they hurled insults at each other all day long and jumped up and down on their respective branches. When a fight broke out between two crows from rival sides, the others would jump up and down and shout encouragement from the sides. Sometimes, a crow would get so involved that it fell off its perch and only remembered to save itself in the nick of time. They were fun to watch, the young ones especially, and after a while I found them a lot less ugly. They were also rather tolerant of other birds I discovered. For hidden amongst the crows was a woodpecker, and two cuckoos. Imagine my joy when one day I glimpsed a brown-headed barbet amongst them!

One day I looked out of the window and saw, to my surprise, a young hawk sitting not far from the crows. It shuffled awkwardly to the right every time a crow came too close, but other than that, it did nothing, staring into space with dejection written into every feather of its young body.

The next day the hawk was still there. This time the other crows weren't so polite either. One bird in particular kept circling around the hawk taking little nips at the bird, which the latter pretended to ignore. I waved at the crow, hoping to scare it away. But by this time the birds were either used to me or they weren't able to see through glass, for neither hawk nor crow paid me the slightest heed.

Birds

Seeing the hawk wasn't retaliating, other crows from the Capulet side (the left hand side, bigger, nastier lot) began to taunt the young hawk. They did it sneakily at first, waiting for the hawk to fall asleep (which it did often as it was obviously weak from hunger). But after a while they stopped bothering to wait and came at the hawk in knots of twos and threes. Each time the hawk just flapped its wings feebly while the crows, cawing with glee, attacked from all sides. I couldn't bear to watch any longer, and so I leaned out and shouted at the crows. This time they noticed and were so surprised that they forgot the hawk.

Then the attacks began again.

It became a game. When I went to the window and shouted the crows stopped attacking the young hawk. Fly away, I silently begged the hawk, next time I may not be able to come in time. But the hawk remained stubbornly where it was, steadily losing feathers and flesh. Afternoon came and went and I grew more and more fearful, until around tea-time...a miracle happened. A medium sized crow suddenly flew to the hawk's defense, attacking the other crows first from the rear and then settling itself beside the hawk, going for the eyes of the other crows with its powerful beak. Taken by surprise the other crows fell back. Luckily I was there when this happened and saw it all.

Eventually the attacks grew fewer and fewer. Night fell and I was forced to turn my attention inwards. The next morning as soon as it was light I was at the window again. Hawk and crow were still there, sitting back to back like Bonnie and Clyde, eyeball to eyeball with the other crows. The hawk seemed a little better, perkier, curious. It hopped up and down the branch, examining things with its beak. Why doesn't it fly away I wondered?

The answer came to me at noon when the heroic crow flew to a nearby dustbin they all enjoyed raiding and returned with something in its beak. It placed what looked like the carcass of a mouse carefully beside the hawk. At first the hawk pretended indifference, then when the crow looked elsewhere it took two short hops and grabbed the morsel of food. Satisfied, the crow flew off to look for something more.

This went on for three days. The hawk just sat there, whilst the crow went off to look for food and fought off fresh attacks. Then on the third day, the hawk unfolded its wings and tried to fly. It didn't get very far, about a foot and half into the air, before the strength seemed to go out of it and it half fell half glided back to its perch.

I was at the window when it happened, and when the

hawk regained its spot I wasn't sure whether to be sad or relieved.

After that, I knew it was only a question of time before the young hawk regained its confidence. So I neglected my work and spent more time at the window watching that strange friendship. If I hadn't seen the way it had happened with my own eyes I wouldn't have thought it possible for a crow to rush to the defense of a hawk. Life was so much stranger than fiction, I thought, unaware that my frequent trips to the window had been noticed by someone.

When the hawk finally flew away I called my parents, elated. After the usual hello, how are you, 'Babuji*,' I said excitedly, 'guess what I saw? A crow protecting a hawk.'

'You what? Who are you talking about? Your neighbour, your boss? A film you saw? I bet it was a film on TV. Don't watch so much TV. You should go out more, meet people your own age,' my father said.

Yes, yes, yes. I held the phone away from my ear and the words blurred, fading slowly into silence. Then the anxious, 'Hello? Are you there beti?'

'Yes.' I say wearily, 'I'm here.'

'Are you eating well? Everything ok? You can always

---

* Babuji: Indian terms of respect

come back if you don't like it.'

'I'm fine.' I put the phone down.

A few months later the old banyan tree gave fruit. And a new lot of birds arrived, mainly parakeets but also six *coppersmith barbets*, to feast on the lovely red fruit. Coppersmith barbets. I could hardly believe my eyes. Smaller than their cousin the brown headed barbet, the coppersmith barbets loved to eat, and all through the day I would see them darting from one cluster of fruit to the next. They were so pretty I couldn't take my eyes off them. Their bodies were the wonderful fresh spring green striped with a darker shade—somewhere between dark blue and dark green—that characterized the entire barbet clan. But their heads were just spectacular. Kohl rimmed eyes were highlighted with a ring of lemon yellow and around that, to make the eyes even more special, some artist had painted another ring of—of dark, dark blue. Shades of turquoise and ultramarine ringed the neck. On its forehead and on the chest was a blaze of pure scarlet. To draw attention to the scarlet dot on the chest, the same unknown artist had put another spot of lemon yellow just above it.

In the morning the birds would sun themselves on the telephone pole in the compound of the neighbouring building. The gentle morning sun did lovely things to their already spectacular colouring. But the barbets were not alone on the telephone pole. They had to fight the sparrows and the parrots. Eventually, the three species found a compromise and space was made for all, even for the few crows who stayed on the telephone line. I mention the other birds because one day I noticed something strange. A crow had settled itself on the arm of the telephone pole where the barbets sat all together. The contrast was really shocking: the barbets, elegant, graceful, petite, and the large crow, gawky, black and vulgar. The barbets seemed equally confused about the crow. But since they were small, there was little they could do except ignore it. But this only seemed to distress the crow further, who ruffled its feathers and made bleak pronouncements on the unfairness of the world in its ugly unmusical voice. The call of the barbets, by contrast, was sweet and bell-like, like someone hitting a copper drum.

Every day the crow would desert its own kind and sit between the barbets, trying to make itself appear smaller than it was, as if this would somehow transform it into one of them. Of course it only made the crow look more ridiculous. But the crow didn't care. It was as besotted by the beauty of the barbets as I was. Towards ten to eleven o'clock, when the barbets flew off to feed and to sun themselves on the topmost branches of the banyan, the crow would reluctantly rejoin its own kind.

On one such day, as I followed the ascent of the barbets with my eyes, I noticed that there was a man at the window of the elegant apartment I liked so much. He was waving and blowing air kisses at me. I leapt away from the window as if it had suddenly become toxic, then I went back and drew the curtains, plunging the room into darkness. My lovely airy apartment had become a glass cage. I had to get out.

Grabbing my keys and handbag, I wrenched open the main door and left.

On the sidewalk, I still felt followed, observed. I walked very fast till I found a barista and entered. Only after I'd ordered my coffee did I realize that my feet had led me to my favourite café, the one with the little outdoor courtyard under a banyan tree. I sat down under the tree. Only one other table was occupied. The coffee and muffin began to take effect. Slowly I relaxed, started pondering ways to deal with my neighbour. I was so caught up in my thoughts that I never noticed the crow until it was too late and my muffin was gone. What's more, the bird was so impudent it didn't go far—landing barely two feet away. Had I not encountered the crow-that-tried-to-be-a-barbet or the hawk's saviour I would have probably thrown something at the crow. But

Birds

because of those other birds, I just watched it rather tolerantly, the way one would a naughty two year old.

'What a naughty bird. Shall I get you another one?' The voice was deep, male, and tolerantly amused. I looked up, words of rejection already forming themselves in my mind.

'They are funny creatures, crows, so ugly, but surprisingly human too.'

'Y...you like them?' I found myself stammering. He was very good-looking, in an easy open cosmopolitan way.

'I'll tell you a true story about crows, a real Bombay story.' He pulled his chair closer. 'There was an old man living in an apartment building like the one above. He was a rich businessman. When he was seventy five, his wife, who was some years younger than him, died. But before dying she made him promise to take her ashes to Banaras. So he left his businesses and home in the charge of his sons, signing powers of attorneys that gave them total control over his wealth, and went off to Banaras. When he returned, he found no one at the station to pick him up and when he arrived at his home, he could not enter. When he tried to call his sons, they wouldn't pick up the phone and his credit cards wouldn't work. He had been turned into a beggar. Eventually an old chaukidar gave him shelter under the stairs. But at 6am the chaukidar awoke him and begged him to leave.

The old man didn't live long on the streets. But whatever he got he shared with the crows and pigeons. Soon the birds all knew him and they would come and perch on his shoulders and eat unafraid out of his hands. When he died, the crows followed his corpse to the cremation ground, and until his body became ash they remained there, mourning him.'

When at last I found my voice I asked, 'How do you know this story?'

'The man was my grandfather,' he replied.

Suddenly I knew what I was going to do. I didn't let myself think. 'You can see the crows up close from my apartment. I watch them all the time. Would you like to come and see them one day?'

Extract from The Wreck of the Zanzibar

by Michael Morpurgo

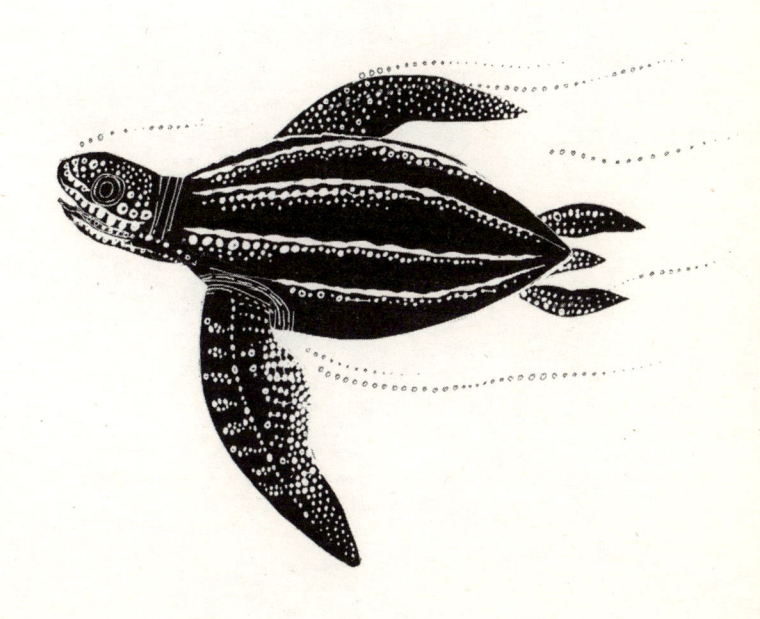

September 8th

TODAY I FOUND A TURTLE I THINK IT'S CALLED a leatherback turtle. I found one once before but it was dead. This one has been washed up alive.

Father had sent me down to collect driftwood on Rushy Bay. He said there'd be plenty about after a storm like that. He was right.

I'd been there for half an hour or so heaping up the wood, before I noticed the turtle in the tide line of piled seaweed. I thought at first he was just a washed-up tree stump covered in seaweed.

He was upside down on the sand. I pulled the seaweed off him. His eyes were open, unblinking. He was more dead than alive, I thought. His flippers were quite still, and held out to the clouds above as if he was worshipping them. He was massive, as long as this bed, and wider. He had a face like a two hundred year old man, wizened and wrinkled and wise with a gently smiling mouth.

I looked around, and there were more gulls gathering. They were silent, watching, waiting; and I knew well enough what they were waiting for. I pulled away more of the seaweed and saw that the gulls had been at him already. There was blood under his neck where the skin

Extract from The Wreck of the Zanzibar

had been pecked. I had got there just in time. I bombarded the gulls with pebbles and they flew off protesting noisily, leaving me alone with my turtle.

I knew it would be impossible to roll him over, but I tried anyway. I could rock him back and forth on his shell, but I could not turn him over, no matter how hard I tried. After a while I gave up and sat down beside him on the sand. His eyes kept closing slowly as if he was dropping off to sleep, or maybe he was dying—I couldn't be sure. I stroked him under his chin where I thought he would like it, keeping my hand well away from his mouth.

A great curling storm wave broke and came tumbling towards us. When it went hissing back over the sand, it left behind a broken spar. It was as if the sea was telling me what to do. I dragged the spar up the beach. Then I saw the turtle's head go back and his eyes closed. I've often seen seabirds like that. Once their heads go back there's nothing you can do. But I couldn't just let him die. I couldn't. I shouted at him. I shook him. I told him he wasn't to die, that I'd turn him over somehow, that it wouldn't be long.

I dug a deep hole in the sand beside him. I would lever him up and topple him in. I drove the spar into the sand underneath his shell. I drove it in again and again, until it was as deep as I could get it. I hauled back on it and felt him shift. I threw all my weight on it and at last he tumbled over into the hole, and the right way up, too. But when I scrambled over to him, his head lay limp in the sand, his eyes closed to the world. There wasn't a flicker of life about him. He was dead. I was quite sure of it now. It's silly, I know—I had only known him for a few minutes—but I felt I had lost a friend.

I made a pillow of soft sea lettuce for his head and knelt beside him. I cried till there were no more tears to cry. And then I saw the gulls were back. They knew too. I screamed at them, but they just glared at me and moved in closer.

'No!' I cried. 'No!'

I would never let them have him, never. I piled a mountain of seaweed on top of him and my driftwood on top of that. The next tide would take him away. I left him and went home.

I went back to Rushy Bay this evening, at high tide, just before nightfall, to see if my turtle was gone. He was still there. The high tide had not been high enough. The gulls were done though, all of them. I really don't know what made me want to see him once more. I pulled the wood and seaweed away until I could see the top of his head. As I looked it moved and lifted. He was blinking up at me. He was alive again! I could have kissed him, really I could. But I didn't quite dare.

Extract from The Wreck of the Zanzibar

He's still there now, all covered up against the gulls, I hope. In the morning...

I had to stop writing because Father just came in. He hardly ever comes in my room, so I knew at once something was wrong.

'You all right?' he said, standing in the doorway. 'What've you been up to?'

'Nothing,' I said, 'Why?'

'Old man Jenkins. He said he saw you down on Rushy Bay.'

'I was just collecting the wood,' I told him, as calmly as I could, 'like you said I should.' I find lying so difficult. I'm just not good at it.

'He thought you were crying, crying your eyes out, he says.'

'I was not,' I said, but I dared not look at him. I pretended to go on writing in my diary.

'You are telling me the truth, Laura?' He knew I wasn't, he knew it.

'Course,' I said. I just wished he would go.

'What do you find to write in that diary of yours?' he asked.

'Things,' I said. 'Just things.'

And he went out and shut the door behind him. He knows something, but he doesn't know what. I'm going to have to be very careful. If Father finds out about the turtle, I'm in trouble. He's only got to go down to Rushy Bay and look. That turtle would just be food to him, and to anyone else who finds him. We're all hungry, everyone is getting hungrier every day. I should tell him. I know I should. But I can't do it. I just can't let them eat him.

In the morning, early, I'll have to get him back into the sea. I don't know how I'm going to do it, but somehow I will. I must. Now it's only the gulls I have to save from him.

September 9th
The Day of the Turtle

I SHALL REMEMBER TODAY AS LONG AS I LIVE. This morning I slipped away as soon as ever I could. No one saw me go and no one followed me, I made quite sure of that. I'd lain awake most of the night wondering how I was going to get my turtle back into the water. But as I made my way down to Rushy Bay, the morning fog lifting off the sea, I had no idea at all how I would do it. Even as I uncovered him, I still didn't know. I only knew it had to be done. So I talked to him. I was trying to explain it all to him, how he mustn't worry, how I'd find a way, but that I didn't yet know what way. He's got eyes that make you think he understands. Maybe he

Extract from The Wreck of the Zanzibar

doesn't but you never know. Somehow, once I'd started talking, I felt it was rude not to go on. I fetched some seawater in my hat and I poured it over him. He seemed to like it, lifting his head into it as I poured. So I did it again and again. I told him all about the storm, about Granny May's roof, about the battered boats, and he looked at me. He was listening.

He was so weak though. He kept trying to move, trying to dig his flippers into the sand, but he hadn't the strength to do it. His mouth kept opening and shutting as if he was gasping for breath.

Then I had an idea. I scooped out a long deep channel all the way down to the sea. I would wait for the tide to come in as far as I could, and when the time came I would ease him down into the channel and he could wade out to sea. As I dug I told him my plan. When I'd finished I lay down beside him, exhausted, and waited for the tide.

I told him then all about Billy, about Joseph Hannibal and the General Lee, and about how I missed Billy so much, all about the cows dying and about how nothing had gone right since the day Billy left. When I looked across at him his eyes were closed. He seemed to be dozing in the sun. I'd been talking to myself.

The gulls never left us alone, not for a minute. They stood eyeing us from the rocks, from the shallows. When I threw stones at them now, they didn't fly off, they just hopped a little further away, and they always came back. I didn't go home for lunch—I just hoped Father wouldn't come looking for me. I couldn't leave my turtle, not with the gulls all around us just waiting for their moment. Besides, the tide was coming in now, close all the time. Then there was barely five yards of sand left between the sea and my turtle, and the water was washing up the channel just as I'd planned it. It was now or never.

I told him what he had to do.

'You've got to walk the rest,' I said. 'You want to get back in the sea, you've got to walk, you hear me?'

He tried. He honestly tried. Time and again he dug the edge of his flippers into the sand, but he just couldn't move himself.

The flippers dug in again, again, but he stayed where he was. I tried pushing him from behind. That didn't work. I tried moving his flippers for him one by one. That didn't work. I slapped his shell. I shouted at him. All he did was swallow once or twice and blink at me. In the end I tried threatening him. I crouched down in front of him.

'All right,' I said. 'All right. You stay here if you like. See if I care. You see those gulls? You know what they're waiting for? If they don't get you, then someone else'll find you and you'll be turtle stew.' I was shouting at him now. I was really shouting at him. 'Turtle stew do you

Extract from The Wreck of the Zanzibar

hear me!' All the while his eyes never left my face, not for a moment. Bullying hadn't worked either. So now I tried begging.

'Please,' I said, 'please.' But his eyes gave me the answer I already knew. He could not move. He hadn't the strength. There was nothing else left to try. From the look in his eyes I think he knew it too.

I wandered some way away from him and sat down on the rock to think. I was still thinking, fruitlessly, when I saw the gig coming around Droppy Nose Point and heading out to sea. Father was there—I recognised his cap. Old Man Jenkins was in Billy's place and the chief was setting the jib sail. They were far too far away to see my turtle. I came back to him and sat down.

'See that gig?' I told him. 'One day I'm going to row in that gig, just like Billy did. One day.'

And I told him all about the gig and the big ships that come into Scilly needing a pilot to bring them in safely, and how the gigs race each other to get out there first. I told him about the wrecks too, and about how the gigs will put to sea in any weather if there's sailors to rescue or cargo to salvage. The strange thing is, I didn't feel at all silly talking to my turtle. I mean, I know it *is* silly, but it just seemed the natural thing to do. I honestly think I told the turtle more about me than I've ever told anyone before. I looked down at him. He was nudging at the sand with his chin, his mouth opening. He was hungry! I don't know why I hadn't thought of it before. I had no idea at all what turtles eat. So I tried what was nearest first—seaweed of all sorts, sea lettuce, bladderwrack, whatever I could find.

I dangled it in front of his mouth, brushing his nose with it so he could smell it. He looked as if he was going to eat it. He opened his mouth slowly and snapped at it. But then he turned his head away and let it fall to the ground.

'What then?' I asked.

A sudden shadow fell across me. Granny May was standing above me in her hat.

'How long have you been there?' I asked.

'Long enough,' she said and she walked around me to get a better look at the turtle.

'Let's try shrimps. We'd better hurry. We don't want anyone else finding him, do we?' And she sent me off home to fetch the shrimping net. I ran all the way there and all the way back, wondering if Granny May knew about her roof yet.

Granny May is the best shrimper on the island. She knows every likely cluster of seaweed on Rushy Bay, and everywhere else come to that. One sweep through the shallows and she was back, her net jumping with shrimps. She smiled down at my turtle.

Extract from The Wreck of the Zanzibar

'Useful, that is,' she said, tapping him with her stick.

'What?' I replied.

'Carrying your house around with you. Can't hardly have your roof blowed off, can you?' So she did know.

'It'll mend,' she said. 'Roofs you can mend easily enough, hope is a little harder.'

She told me to dig out a bowl in the sand, right under the turtle's chin, and then she shook out her net. He looked mildly interested for a moment then looked away. It was no good. Granny May was looking out to sea, shielding her eyes against the glare of the sun.

'I wonder,' she murmured. 'I wonder. I shan't be long.' And she was gone, down to the sea. She was wading out up to her ankles, then up to her knees, her shrimping net scooping through the water around her. I stayed behind with the turtle and threw more stones at the gulls. When she came back, her net was bulging with jellyfish, blue jellyfish. She emptied them into the turtle's sandy bowl. At once he was at them like a vulture, snapping, crunching, swallowing, until there wasn't a tentacle left.

'He's smiling,' she said. 'I think he likes them. I think perhaps he'd like some more.'

'I'll do it,' I said. I picked up the net and rushed off down into the sea. They were not difficult to find. I've never liked jellyfish, not since I was stung on my neck when I was little and came out in a burning weal that lasted for months. So I kept a wary eye around me. I scooped up twelve big ones in as many minutes. He ate those and then lifted his head, asking for more. We took it in turns after that, Granny May and me, until at last he seemed to have had enough and left a half-chewed jellyfish lying there, the shrimps still hopping all around it. I crouched down and looked my turtle in the eye.

'Feel better now?' I asked, and I wondered if turtles burp when they've eaten too fast. He didn't burp, but he did move. The flippers dug deeper. He shifted—just a little at first. And then he was scooping himself slowly forward, inching his way through the sand. I went loony. I was cavorting up and down like a wild thing, and Granny May was just the same. The two of us whistled and whooped to keep him moving, but we knew soon enough that we didn't need to. Every step he took was stronger, his neck reaching forward purposefully. Nothing would stop him now. As he neared the sea, the sand was tide-ribbed and wet, and he moved ever faster, faster, past the rock pools and across the muddy sand where the lungworms leave their curly casts. His flippers were under the water now. He was half walking, half swimming. Then he dipped his snout into the sea and let the water run over his head and down his neck. He was going, and

Extract from The Wreck of the Zanzibar

suddenly I didn't want him to. I was alongside him, bending over him.

'You don't have to go,' I said.

'He wants to,' said Granny May. 'He has to.'

He was in deeper water now, and with a few powerful strokes he was gone, cruising out through the turquoise water of the shallows to the deep blue beyond. The last I saw of him he was a dark shadow under the sea making out towards Samson.

I felt suddenly alone. Granny May knew it I think, because she put her arm around me and kissed the top of my head.

Back at home we never said a word about our turtle. It wasn't an arranged secret, nothing like that. We just didn't tell anyone because we didn't want to—it was private somehow.

Father says he'll try to make a start on her house tomorrow, just to keep the weather out. Granny May doesn't seem at all interested.

She just keeps smiling at me, confidentially. Mother knows something is going on between us, but she doesn't know what. I'd like to tell her, but I can't talk to her like I used to.

If Billy were here I'd tell him.

I haven't thought about Billy today and I should have. All I've thought about is my turtle. If I don't think about Billy I'll forget him, and then it'll be as if he was never here at all, as if I never had a brother, as if he never existed, and if he never existed then he can't come back, and he must. He must.

This is the longest day I've ever written in my diary and all because of a turtle. My wrist aches.

The Morning After

by Polly Samson

They were all there, the plump men in their dickie-bows, the women glinting with sequins and spite, rattling their jewels at one another and casting acquisitive eyes over the list of auction items for later. The usual things were up for grabs: the golf weekends and wing-walking opportunities that would be re-donated to another charity as soon as the winning bidder sobered up, the dinners at expensive restaurants hungry for promotion, the handbags donated by designers fashionably doing their bit for the environment, for the fluffier of God's soon-to-be extinct creatures, for children, for Africans, for whatever.

Olivia felt at home on the usual spindly gold chair, her breasts nestling in her dress, displayed for all the world like a couple of Easter eggs in novelty egg cups. She milked her friend Sabrina for the grislier details of a recent weekend in Gloucestershire to which Olivia had not been invited.

'...and the children! The girl—who is not a looker, by the way—wouldn't let Julia finish a single sentence and the boy had to be sent to his room for slipping worms onto the barbeque.'

'Oh yuck...' Ever since she'd been widowed Olivia had found herself left off the guest lists of all the jolly occasions. She took it as affirmation of her own attractiveness in the eyes of the other wives.

The croustade of quails eggs came and went, the man on her left sloshed Pouilly Fume into her glass. 'Not such a bad vintage,' he said with yolk yellowing the cracks at the corners of his mouth. Olivia rather hoped he wasn't so well brought up that he'd feel impelled to turn away from his companion to make conversation with her for the duration of the next course, which was, quite predictably, to be salmon.

'They only discovered what he'd been doing with the worms after everyone had eaten their lamb burgers,' Sabrina was saying. 'Revolting. I was nearly sick.' She waved a hand at the floral arrangement in the centre of the table: 'Why do you suppose they always put things like vegetables in there? Artichokes? Are they trying to surprise us?' dismissing the flowers while Olivia watched the diamonds flare at her wrist. 'Mistress present,' said Sabrina catching her eye. 'So much better than anything he ever bought me after we were married.'

The pudding, a concoction of white chocolate mousse and crushed raspberries in a gilded cage of spun sugar, was left untouched by both women. The man who had been so enthusiastically refilling her wine glass claimed to have once been a drummer in a rock band. She and Sabrina found him just a little bit interesting after that.

As the coffee and petit fours arrived a woman whose Minnie Mouse voice rendered her unsuitable for public speaking took to the podium to introduce the guest speaker. 'It is because of people like Daniel Flint that the trade in Indian Tiger products has been brought to light,' she squeaked. A juddery video was being shown of tiger skins being shaken out on dusty streets. The swerving camera picked out a shelf of bottles. Chinese characters in gold, a translation in bold type, and no, it wasn't a mistake: "Tiger wine" printed on the labels.

'Oh, how awful,' Sabrina said, reaching for a tiny square of fudge and then thinking better of it, as a tall man with shoulder length dark curls bounded on to the stage.

'Who's that? Lord Byron?' said the drummer but the women were not listening to him any more.

Daniel Flint spoke in a voice as rich and dark as pure Arabica. His surveillance team had taken many risks concealing cameras in brief cases, posing as businessmen, meeting the illegal traders late at night and bringing back footage that more than hinted at corruption and links to government agencies.

'I know that you're here to have a good time and straight after the auction the band will be on but I ask you please not to ignore the envelopes that have been placed on the tables before you,' he said, and before he had finished speaking Olivia was unsnapping her bag,

The Morning After

which was too small to hold a chequebook, hoping her credit card would do. 'Your donations will make a difference.' Daniel Flint seemed to look straight at her and she felt herself grow hot. 'Your donations will fund our work to expose this illegal trade.' And then, still looking at her he thumped the lectern: 'If we don't act now the Indian Tiger will be wiped off our planet within the next decade.'

Oh it was shameful! By the following evening, the artichokes that Daniel Flint had salvaged from the floral arrangements were bobbing about in a pan of salted water in Olivia's Holland Park kitchen, and they were both still laughing as she opened the second bottle of wine.

He had noticed her almost immediately: she was hard to miss with that hair and those legs. He had picked out the drummer whose band had provided the soundtrack to his youth, and there she was staring up at him with huge doe eyes, twisted around in her chair, blonde hair lustrous around her shoulders and falling in thick waves against the emerald sheen of her dress.

She's wearing a loose silk blouse this evening. Her amber eyes glisten, he sees tears wobble and spill as he tells her about the things he's seen. The carcasses: so many of them. The bones with bits of tiger skin still attached that are suspended in the bottles of rice wine. 'Like the worms in tequila,' she says, twisting her hair.

'Much worse.'

'Oh yes, I didn't mean that...'

He reaches over and touches the sweet tip of her nose where a little butter has made it shine. 'And the tiger's nose leather is used to treat wounds,' he says. His fingers move to the top of her head. 'The brain is ground into a paste for pimples.' He kneels at her feet, takes her hands in his. 'The claws are used to cure insomnia...' Her nails are lacquered bright red and he kisses them one by one. She smells deliciously of aniseed.

She woke shivering from the strangest dream. Daniel Flint lay stretched out beside her, one arm thrown across the pillow, palm upwards as though waiting for something to be placed into it, the other lost beneath the sheets. He was smiling slightly in his sleep in a way that made her envy whatever was going on in there. Her own dream hadn't been so bad, just odd: she had been tiptoeing through the snow on a high silvery plateau, wrapped in soft furs, a tiny fawn-like creature on wobbly legs beside her, nibbling and nuzzling her, looking up at her with liquid brown eyes, and in the dream she knew that this was her baby, and that just out of sight Daniel was standing, sniffing the air for danger, guarding them. She steals another look at him across her pillow: his nostrils flare slightly, his eyelashes and brows are so dark they appear to have been sketched and smudged on to his face with charcoal. It seems impossible that such a beautiful specimen is lying in her bed. It's like finding a Faberge egg in a junk shop.

She tiptoes from the bed. Moonlight floods the room as she slides back the curtains and she can smell the night-scented jasmine that winds its way from the garden to her window, but still she can't shake her chill. Daniel stirs slightly in his sleep, mutters something that sounds like "beloved," and turns his face into the pillow. Olivia can't stop smiling as she wraps herself in her shahtoosh and wonders at her strange dream. How can it be that a mere vision of a snowy wasteland can make her feel so cold on a summer's night?

She slips back into bed, shivering despite the shawl, her beloved "toosh" given to her on her wedding night, and the envy of all her friends. The fine faun-coloured cloth so wondrous it was said that a pigeon egg would hatch if it were to be wrapped in it. 'There,' her husband ran the miraculous bolt right through the centre of her wedding ring. 'The real thing. I won't tell you how much it cost.'

Daniel wakes with a dry mouth and Olivia's sheets tangled around his legs. He reaches for her across the bed and his fingers snag against something soft. He slides his eyes sideways and even in the pinkish dawn he fears that he knows only too well what it is she has wrapped around herself.

He turns onto his elbow and gingerly rubs a piece of the cloth between his finger and thumb: it is unmistakably a shahtoosh, made from hairs so fine that whoever wove it had probably gone blind.

A small snore escapes from Olivia's mouth, and with it a sour smell. Stupid woman! He doesn't know if he wants to shout at her or run away. Both probably. He wonders if she's one of the brainless ones who believe these things were fashioned from the shed breast feathers of the fictitious Tooshi bird, but doubts it. The newspapers have been full of this fashion scandal: the massacre of four young Chiru antelopes for every shawl. He stands from the bed and bends down over her, just to be sure. He should wake her up and tell her how the chirus died for her: caught in the headlights and gunned down, or with their legs bitten through by the teeth of a barbarous trap. He should tell her how soon these beautiful creatures will become extinct and how it will be a double tragedy since the chiru's fleeces are carried over the mountains to the Indian border and bartered for Tiger parts: India trading with China so that every shahtoosh has the blood of a tiger upon it. But the nausea he feels is rising from his stomach and burning his throat and she doesn't smell so good to him now. A breeze sucks at the curtain and shadows fall across her face.

The Morning After

She had seemed almost radiant to him the night before, with her trembling tears and righteous indignation; he would have been happy to die in her arms; but now he can see that it was all artifice. If he tugged hard enough the blonde tresses would probably come off in his hands and there is something unnatural about the curve of her cheek, in the tightness of her jaw and in the way her brow remains mysteriously untroubled. He grabs his things, leaving her lying beneath her shroud, and finds his way out and into the morning.

A Dream of Cranes

by Nirmal Ghosh

Maya's father was a farmer in India. Before inheriting land from his father, he had been a boatman on the Jamuna river. From its glacier at Yamunotri, high in the icy Himalayas, the Jamuna snakes across the lower plains of tropical heat and the deluge of monsoon rains and cold, cold winters, past the city of Agra and behind the shining Taj Mahal.

The Taj Mahal was built long ago, but the river had been there for a long long time even before that. It only changed course a little bit each year, determined by the monsoon rains. The rains always came after a hot dry summer, to flush the land and turn it green again.

Every day Maya's father would pole his boat full of people across the Jamuna.

He had been friends then, with another boatman he referred to as Pagla Baba—the mad babaji: one of the Hindu mystics who roam alone with no material possessions.

Pagla Baba had given up his boat to wander the land. But years later he came to their house one day to meet his friend. Maya had heard her father Abhijit talk about him. But it was the first time Maya had seen him.

He was a lean man, naked from the waist up, so wiry you could see his veins and muscles. His body was a burnt coffee brown, his hair hung in dreadlocks. He carried a simple jute bag over his shoulder and had worn sandals on his feet. He wore just a sarong, with a shawl for the cold.

He had a beard, as matted as his hair. He had a hook of a nose and furrows on his brow. But it was his eyes that fascinated Maya. They were large, dark brown and bright, with a wild crazy light in them.

Maya was only six years old then. He looked at her face with a knowing glint and nodded as if he had understood something. Then he suddenly laughed and said,

'What are you doing here little one? You do not belong with us. You have the soul of a Sarus crane, you belong with them. You'd better stay free like them when you grow up!'

He gave her a closer and more intense look, and then laughed again, saying 'Hahh! You think I'm joking, huh? Remember, there is nothing you cannot do if you follow your dreams!'

He leaned forward, his face suddenly gentle and kind. Placing his hands on Maya's shoulders he said to her, 'Freedom.'

She was thinking about this later as she drifted off to sleep. The two men, Pagla Baba and her father, talked quietly on the other side of the wall. In their tiny house with the white paint now yellowed and peeling, the old electric fan whirred quietly in a corner, pushing out the still muggy air. Frogs croaked in the rice paddies outside.

She woke in the silence of the pre-dawn darkness. It seemed that a tap on the window had woken her, but she could not be sure. She sat up and looked out at the starlit night. She saw the silhouette of two big birds, very close to the house.

She got out of bed and went outside, carefully and quietly opening and closing the door.

It was autumn and a cold fog lay across the endless rice fields. In winter the farmers here plant wheat and mustard, but through the monsoon and into autumn, as far as the eye can see there are rice fields, their green stalks shifting like waves in the wind. Sometimes the wind seems to play with them, carving S shapes. Sometimes it just roars across the rice in a straight line, especially in the monsoon season, and the rice stalks bend until it seems like a flat green road is opening up in the endless plains.

She walked to the edge of their land balancing easily on the narrow bundhs which separated the rice fields. There she saw the Sarus cranes standing in the water. She stepped off the bundh and into the water that reached up to her waist. The cold bit into her legs and suddenly she was really wide awake. She walked slowly through the water, wading across the muddy bottom, towards the cranes.

A Dream of Cranes

One of them, the male, was standing on one foot. 'How do you do that?' she said. He looked at her solemnly, the rising sun catching the colour of his red eyes. He moved his elegant purple head sideways to look down at her.

'It's easy if you know how, I've been doing it since I was born', he said.

Maya tried to lift one leg up and balance but it was difficult, especially in the cold water. She almost fell.

The crane's eyes glinted and he spread his wings briefly. He seemed to be laughing.

To Maya who was much shorter than him, his wings were enormous, almost blocking out the sky.

'What's your name?' she said to him.

'My name is Earth,' he said. 'Her name is Sky,' he added, looking at his mate, who was at the edge of a huge tangled circle of twigs and grass floating on the water. Inside were two big eggs. Sky was bent over the nest, repositioning the eggs with her long beak. She looked up briefly at Maya and said: 'And our next child is going to be called Water.'

'But there are two eggs,' said Maya.

'Well we haven't decided on the second one's name yet,' said Sky a bit impatiently, as she walked on to the nest and slowly lowered herself into it, settling herself on to the eggs.

Earth looked at Maya.

'Maybe you can help me, I have been meaning to try and find out what these things are all about,' he said, glancing up with a tilt of his head. He looked towards the huge electricity pylons and the thick cables they held, that walked across the land like giants.

'They are for electricity,' said Maya proudly. 'For the big hydro electric project to the north.' She had asked her parents what they were when the workmen were putting them up just a few months ago.

'What's that?' said Earth.

She thought for a while and then said, 'To get light. To read at night. For heat when it gets cold. And a fan when it gets hot.'

And she thought for a while more and said 'For the TV!'

'Huh?' said the crane. 'TV? What's that?'

'It's something like a box, and you can see moving pictures and drawings and see and hear people talking, with music and all,' she said.

'Hmm, interesting,' he said, and she could tell from his voice that he was getting bored.

'Maybe I should leave,' Maya thought. She stretched and bounced on her toes, and flapped her wings. She had wings! Something had happened.

With strong, rapid wing beats she powered up into the sky, now beginning to lighten with the first pale pink streaks of the rising sun. She wheeled above the green rice fields, looking down at Earth and Sky who were glancing up at her anxiously.

Sky left the nest. Stretching her neck and throwing back her head she gave a piercing bugling call. Maya answered. Then Earth and Sky ran a few steps and took flight as well. They came up to meet her, flying alongside.

She could hear the wind whistle through their pinions, and through her own. She experimented with the wind; facing into it and soaring; getting above it and gliding; riding warm rising thermals as the sun stirred the air.

Earth and Sky just circled nearby, anxiously it seemed. But soon they came and flew alongside. They chirped at her and she knew it was time to go down.

As she glided down, she heard screams and a sickening thud behind her. The fright unbalanced her and flapping in alarm, she pulled up and around. She saw with horror Earth and Sky lying crumpled in the rice field below the huge electricity pylon.

She flew down, her heart cold with dread. The two big birds lay next to each other, their beautiful long necks now running with fresh bright blood. Their wings were broken and trailed uselessly as they tried to stand up. They fell repeatedly. The strength drained out of their hearts and the glow in their eyes grew dimmer and dimmer.

She stayed with them through the night. In the morning

when she awoke, she cried aloud as she saw them lifeless at her feet. Her cries woke the people in the nearby house. As they ran towards her she moved away, half flying and half walking. They gathered around the corpses of the two adult Sarus cranes shaking their heads in sorrow.

Maya suddenly woke up, the cold of the autumn morning on her face. Her mother hurried out anxiously, sweeping her up in a warm shawl. 'What are you doing out here?' she asked nuzzling her neck.

'I was dreaming,' she said. 'About the big birds. About the Sarus cranes. And they died.' She was sobbing as her mother led her into the house.

'Why did they die?' asked her mother, whose name was Amrita.

'Because they hit the wire,' she said, turning around and pointing at the big pylons stalking across the fields with the heavy cables sagging between them.

'Oh but they are ok,' said Amrita, picking her up and cradling her. 'See?' and she pointed into the distance and Maya saw the two big birds now more visible in the lifting mist.

'Oh so they are not dead?' said Maya, peering at them.

'They are not dead, they are fine,' said Amrita.

'But they can die if they hit the wires?' said Maya.

Amrita sighed. 'Yes, they can die if they hit the wires,' she said.

A Dream of Cranes

'Can you ask them to take the wires away then please,' said Maya, and she began to cry again, the tears welling into her eyes and her little chest heaving.

'I will, I will,' said Amrita, holding Maya close. Her father was up by then and had hurried out and heard what Maya had said. Pagla Baba had also heard her. He laughed and turned to Abhijit saying, 'Hah! What did I tell you?'

Abhijit smiled.

'Come in and have some hot chai,' he said to them. 'Come inside, and I will tell you what I am going to do.'

As the big old blackened kettle heated on the wood fire, Abhijit took Maya onto his lap and said, 'I am the headman of our village. That means people listen to me. And I promise at our next meeting, I will get everyone to agree to talk to the government about the wires. I will do something to help the cranes.'

Maya nodded, only barely understanding but knowing that her father would do something for the birds.

They all drank tea as the sun came up and the mist lifted. She walked outside and saw the great birds. Suddenly they started running. They took to the air with strong wing beats and circled up into the sky.

She saw them coming towards her, gliding slowly, side-by-side, wing tip to giant wing tip. They landed gently in front of her. Earth said, 'Thank you Maya.'

And Sky said, 'Will you come and see us again sometime?'

'Yes' said Maya. Then with powerful wing beats they lifted off, disappearing into the sky in a great arc.

Abhijit came running out then. 'What are you doing Maya?' he said anxiously. 'What happened?'

'Nothing,' she said as she turned and walked back into the house with him.

And quietly, to herself, she smiled.

The Seahorse
and the Reef

by Witi Ihimaera

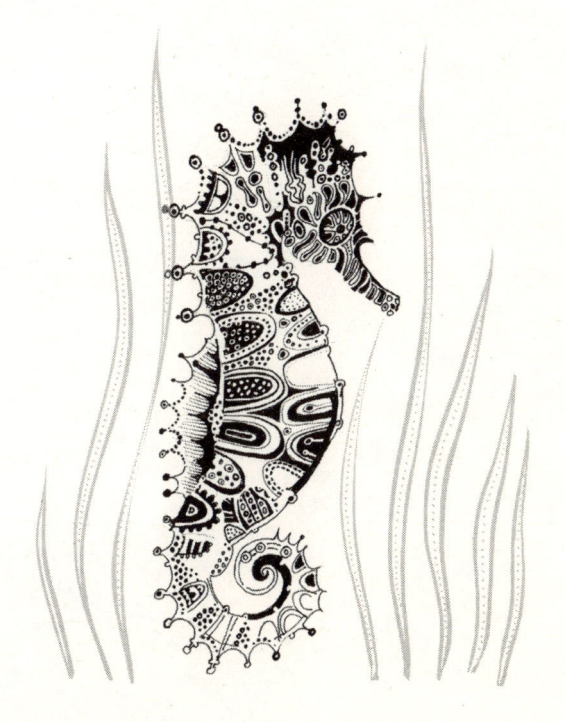

Sometimes through the soft green water and drifting seaweed of my dreams, I see the seahorse again. Delicate and fragile it comes to me, shimmering and luminous with light. And I remember the reef.

The reef was just outside the town where my family lived. That was a long time ago, when I was a boy, before I came to this southern city. It was where all our relatives and friends went every weekend in the summer to dive for kai moana[*]. The reef was the home of much kai moana— paua, pipi, kina, mussels, pupu and many other shellfish. It was the home too of other fish like flounder and octopus. It teemed with life and food. It gave its bounty to us. It was good to us.

And it was where the seahorse lived.

At that time our family lived in a small wooden house on the fringe of the industrial estate. On Sundays my father would watch out the window and see our relatives passing by on their old trucks and cars or bikes with their sugarbags and nets, their flippers and goggles, shouting and waving on their way to the

---

[*] Maori word for Seafood.

The Seahorse and the Reef

reef. They came from the pa—in those days it was not surrounded by expanding suburbia—and they would sing out to Dad:

'Hey, Rongo! Come on! Good day for kai moana today!'

Dad would sigh and start to moan and fidget. The lunch dishes had to be washed, the lawn had to be cut, and my mother probably would want him to do other things around the house.

But after a while, a gleam would come into his eyes.

'Hey, Huia!' he would shout to Mum. 'Those kina are calling out loud to me today!'

'So are these dishes,' she would answer.

'Well, Mum!' Dad would call again. 'Those paua are just waiting for me to come to them today!'

'That lawn's been waiting even longer,' Mum would answer.

Dad would pretend not to hear her. 'Pare kare, dear! How would you like a feast of mussels today!'

'I'd like it better if you fixed the fence,' she would growl.

So Dad would just wiggle his toes and act sad for her. 'Okay, Huia. But those pipi.' And sure enough she would answer him:

'What are we waiting for! Can't disappoint those pipi today!' Then she would shout to us to get into our bathing clothes, grab some sugarbags, don't forget knives and take your time *but hurry up*! And off we would go to the reef on our truck.

If it was a sunny day the reef would already be crowded with people searching for kai moana. There they'd be, dotting the water with their sacks and flax kits. They would wave and shout to us and we would hurry to join them, pulling on our shoes, grabbing our sugarbags and running down to the sea.

'Don't you kids come too far out!' Dad would yell. He would already be way ahead of us, sack clutched in one hand, a knife in the other. He used the knife to prise the paua from the reef because if you weren't quick enough they held on to the rocks really tight. Sometimes, Dad would put on a diving mask. It made it easier for him to see underwater.

As for Mum, she liked nothing better than to wade out to where some of the women of the pa were gathered. Then she would korero with them while she was looking for seafood. Throughout the long afternoon those women would bend to the task, their dresses ballooning above the water, and talk and talk and talk and *talk*.

For both Mum and Dad, much of the fun of going to the reef was because they could be with their friends and whanau. It was a good time to be a family again and to enjoy our family ways.

The Seahorse and the Reef

My sisters and I made straight for a special place on the reef that we liked to call "ours". It was where the pupu—or winkles as some call them—crawled.

We called the special place our pupu pool.

The pool was very long but not very deep. Just as well because Mere, my youngest sister then, would have drowned: she was so short! As for me, the water came only waist high. The rock surrounding the pool was fringed with long waving seaweed. Small transparent fish swam along the waving leaves. Little crabs scurried across the dark floor. The many pupu glided calmly along the sides of the pool. Once, a starfish inched its way into a dark crack.

It was in the pool we discovered the seahorse, magical and serene, shimmering among the red kelp and riding the swirls of the sea's current.

My sisters and I, we wanted to take it home.

'If you take it from the sea it will die,' Dad told us, 'leave it here in its own home for the sea gives it life and beauty.'

Dad told us that we must always treat the sea with love, with aroha*. 'Kids, you must take from the sea

---

* Aroha is a Maori word with many layers of meaning. The light translation is love or a quality that is essential to the survival and total well-being of the world community.

only the kai you need and only the amount you need to please your bellies. If you take more, then it is waste. There is no need to waste the food of the sea. Best to leave it there for when you need it next time. The sea is good to us. If, in your search for shellfish, you lift a stone from its lap, return the stone to where it was. Try not to break pieces of the reef for it is the home of many kai moana. And do not leave litter behind you when you leave the sea.' Dad taught us to respect the sea and to have reverence for the life contained in its waters. As we collected shellfish we would remember his words. Whenever we saw the seahorse shimmering behind a curtain of kelp, we felt glad we'd left it in the pool to continue to delight us.

As soon as we filled our sugar bags we would return to the beach. We played together with other kids while we waited for our parents to return from the outer reef. One by one they would arrive: the women still talking, the men carrying their sacks over their shoulders. On the beach we would laugh and talk and share the kai moana between the different families. With sharing there was little waste. We would be happy with each other unless a stranger intervened with his camera or curious amusement. Then we would say goodbye to one another while the sea whispered and gently surged into the coming darkness.

The Seahorse and the Reef

'See you next weekend,' we would say.

One weekend we went to the reef again. We were in a happy mood. The sun was shining and skipping its beams like bright stones across the water.

But when we arrived at the beach the sea was empty. There were no families. No people dotted the reef with their sacks. No calls of welcome drifted across the rippling waves.

Dad frowned. He looked ahead to where our friends and whanau were clustered in a large lost group on the sand. All of them were looking to the reef, their faces etched by the sun with impassiveness.

'Something's wrong,' Dad said. He stopped the truck. We walked with him towards the other people. They were silent. 'Is the water too cold?' Dad tried to joke.

Nobody answered him. 'Is there a shark out there?' Dad asked again.

Again there was silence. Then someone pointed to a sign.

'It must have been put up last night,' a man told Dad.

Dad elbowed his way through the crowd to read it.

'Dad, what does it say?' I asked.

His fists were clenched and his eyes were angry. He said one word, explosive and shattering the silence, disturbing the gulls who screamed and clattered about us.

'Rongo,' Mum scolded him.

'First the land and now our food,' Dad said to her.

'What does it say?' I asked again.

His fists were unclenched and his eyes became sad. 'It is dangerous to take seafood from the reef, son.'

'Why, Dad?'

'The sea is polluted, son. If we eat the seafood, we may get sick.'

My sisters and I were silent for a while. 'No more pupu, Dad?'

'No more, pupu.'

I clutched his arm frantically, 'And the seahorse, Dad? The seahorse, will it be all right?'

But he did not seem to hear me.

We walked back to the truck. Behind us, an old woman began to sing a tangi to the reef. It was a very sad song for such a beautiful day. 'Aue... Aue...'

With the rest of the iwi*, we bowed our heads. While she was singing, the sea boiled yellow with liquid waste gushing out from a pipe on the seabed. The stain curled like fingers around the reef.

Then the song was finished. Dad looked out to the reef and called to it in a clear voice.

'Sea, we have been unkind to you. We have poisoned the land and now we feed our poison into your waters.

---

* Maori word for people/tribe/clan.

The Seahorse and the Reef

We have lost our aroha for you and our respect for your life. Forgive us friend.'

We started the truck. We turned homeward.

In my mind I caught a sudden vision of many pupu crawling among polluted rocks. I saw a starfish encrusted with ugliness.

And flashing through dead waving seaweed was a beautiful seahorse, fragile and dream-like, searching frantically for clean and crystal waters.

Camp K 101

by William Boyd

It's ironic, Jurgen Kiel thought to himself—and then wondered if "ironic" were the right word. It was "unusual", certainly; "unforeseen" definitely. Because, when Jurgen Kiel joined the German army he never expected to be posted to Africa, far less the medium-sized provincial town of Min'Jalli in the Democratic People's Republic of Douala. Yet here he was sitting in a watchtower five metres above the beaten earth compound of Camp K 101, three clicks out of Min'Jalli, guarding, to the best of his ability, some 5,000 tonnes of rice, powdered milk, millet seeds and assorted other cereals. He sighed, took off his pale blue UN helmet, and rubbed his short hair vigorously. Of course he was not alone: the squad of UN German soldiers was supported by squads of UN Spanish and Pakistani soldiers. They took turns to guard the camp and provided armed escorts for the convoys of NGO lorries that went out to the food distribution centres in other parts of the DPR of Douala. They were well fed, the civil war was taking place many hundreds of kilometres away and the local population was more than pleased to have a UN base in their town. He was doing good, he supposed, in a vague kind of way, though guarding sacks of rice wasn't exactly the main reason why he had joined the German army. Perhaps it was ironic, after all.

Camp K 101

The African dusk was beginning its short but spectacular duration, the light becoming first a heavy, tarnished gold and then swiftly a muddy orange before the darkness arrived like a door slamming. Already the perimeter lights of Camp K were glowing brightly in the gloom. Jurgen stood and switched on the powerful searchlight in his watchtower overlooking the main gate and the road to Min'Jalli. The road ran alongside a small creek that also formed the boundary to the forest. Jurgen swung the beam across the creek and ran the white circle of light along the treeline. If anyone was coming to pilfer they would arrive from the forest. The creek was low—you could wade across it, cut the barbed wire, slip into the camp, steal a sack or two of rice. It didn't happen very often but as Colonel Kwame, the commandant of Camp K 101, regularly insisted, it was the 'ostentation of vigilance that is our best defence.' Hence the two watchtowers with the .50 calibre machine guns and powerful searchlights. Hence the randomly-timed intra-perimeter patrols through the night. Sometimes they caught pilferers—a terrified boy from the bush, naked and starving; three women with their babies looking for powdered milk—but Camp K 101 was new, the barbed wire fence was dense, taut, tall and well lit. It was very hard to get into.

Jurgen ran the searchlight beam back again. This

banal vista of a little corner of African landscape had become as familiar to him as the view from his back bedroom in his mother's house in Waldbach: there was the bamboo grove, there was the footbridge, there was the giant Mungu fig tree, then trees, more trees, more trees. He switched his light off and called up Stefan in the other watchtower at the other end of the camp on the walkie-talkie.

'K2 all clear,' he said.

'Copy that,' Stefan said. Jurgen could imagine him writing it down in the log book for Colonel Kwame. Operation Ostentatious Vigilance was underway.

Two hours later, Jurgen climbed down from the watchtower, unslung his Koch-Noedler PMG and flicked off the safety, and wandered through the camp amongst the sack-mountains and the corrugated-iron warehouses. When he reached the fence he flipped down his night vision device on his helmet and looked out at a world turned green. The open ground between the camp and the creek glowed a fuzzy pistachio, the creek was olive and the trees of the forest beyond were dark, shadowy emerald, shifting and pulsing as the branches moved in the night breezes. Jurgen clicked on his walkie-talkie and reported in to Stefan. All clear.

Jurgen walked up the wire to the western corner of the camp—ostentatiously—and thumbed-up the cover of his PMG's night-sight. Arms had to be carried visibly, practically flourished, Colonel Kwame had insisted. Yeah, yeah: flourish, brandish, waggle, show... Jurgen froze. Something was moving in the trees on the other side of the creek. He ran to the watchtower and climbed up. He had powerful night-vision binoculars there, mounted on a tripod. He swivelled the lenses, focussed. There, flitting amongst the pale lemon branches of the bamboo grove, was a figure, crouched over, hesitant. Jurgen zoomed the lenses, and chuckled. A goddam monkey! Jesus!

He watched it for a while as it searched the leaves under the Mungu fig. Too large for a monkey—this was a chimpanzee. A chimp with a limp, Jurgen said to himself, as he noticed that one leg was shorter than the other, minus a foot, in fact—no right foot, just a short stump under the knee. The chimp slung itself up into the fig looking for fruit. Jurgen thought about switching on the searchlight and frightening it away but, what the hell, he thought, if he can find any figs left in that tree good luck to him.

He kept the binoculars on zoom and after a minute or two watched the chimp lower itself to the ground. He was a big shaggy beast, Jurgen saw, and the hair on his chin was lighter, as if it was grey. A grey goatee. Like Ludger, his mother's fat boyfriend. So he christened the chimp 'Ludger', there and then. It made him smile—he'd look forward to telling Ludger this story when he went back home to Waldbach at Christmas on leave. Hey Ludger, I called a big old chimpanzee in Africa after you. Why? I wonder: perhaps something about him reminded me of you, fatso...

The next night, Jurgen watched as Ludger the chimp returned to the Mungu tree. There must be the odd fig remaining or fallen, Jurgen thought, to draw him back. Ludger spent hardly any time in the tree, he seemed to find a few figs or remains of figs in the leaf-fritter on the ground. Jurgen zoomed in on the leg-stump. How did you lose your foot, Ludger? A snare? Maybe he stood on a mine? The rebels had laid the odd minefield around their forest camps when they held the territory here a couple of years ago. Jurgen noticed Ludger never put his weight on the stump—maybe it was still sore.

Two days later, when Jurgen knew the rota had come round again for him to be on guard all night in the watchtower, he took six bananas and an old enamel cooking pot and crossed the creek by the foot bridge, making for the Mungu tree. He put the bananas on the ground and upended the cooking pot on top of them, checking that he would have a clear sightline from his watchtower. Ludger was in for a treat tonight.

And sure enough, an hour or so after dark, he saw Ludger limp out of the bamboo grove and head for the

Mungu tree. He went straight for the cooking pot—it must have smelt good—and threw it brusquely away. Jurgen zoomed in, watching him eat the bananas, skin and all. You'll be back, Jurgen thought, now you know how to play the game.

And so it progressed, nightly for the next ten days, whether Jurgen was on watch or patrol or not: at some stage in the day he placed a cache of bananas under the cooking pot beneath the Mungu tree and each morning the bananas would be gone. Jurgen didn't see Ludger retrieve his bounty every time he was on duty in the watchtower but each day's return to the Mungu tree made it obvious that the nightly bounty had been discovered.

And then on the tenth day Jurgen lifted up the cooking pot and saw that last night's bananas had been untouched. He frowned, added the new supply and moved the pot to a slightly more prominent position, kicking away the leaves around it so that it sat in a patch of clear ground. That night he was in the watchtower but saw nothing. The next morning he checked—the bananas had been untouched again. He left them there, just in case. He and some of the Spaniards had been assigned a two-day NGO run up to the northern provincial town of Kitali. Maybe Ludger was unwell—or had moved on. He found himself obscurely troubled, as if the relationship had been unwittingly compromised in some way. Maybe Ludger had become sick of bananas and had been hoping for some figs...?

All the way up to Kitali and back he found himself wondering vaguely what could have happened, running through various uninformed scenarios. Was Ludger part of a nomadic tribe of chimpanzees? Had his injured leg made him a pariah figure? Had his leg become worse...? It was pointless speculating. The empty convoy stopped in Min'Jalli before returning to Camp K and the soldiers were allowed to go to the market. Ludger was looking for some carvings or nick-knacks he could take home to his mother and his sister in Waldbach – souvenirs of his African tour of duty. The six UN soldiers, big in their packs and helmets, their PMGs slung across their fronts, wandered grandly through the market stalls handing out sweets and chewing gum to the hordes of kids who surrounded them. Their interpreter, Jean-Francois, swore at the children, spat in their faces, slapped and kicked them away, but the crowd never diminished, and the soldiers kept giving away sweets.

Then Jurgen stopped. He was in the butchery area of the market. Hacked thin boney joints of meat hung from the rafters of low shacks. Mammies waved palm fronds to keep the flies off. Three kids in ragged shorts sat in front of some liana and cane cages containing small deer and in another cage was a large potto, blinking

Camp K 101

uncomprehendingly in the sunlight. Jurgen called Jean-Francois over. This was another problem. The lingua franca of the PDR of Douala was French—you had to speak English to Jean-Francois (nobody spoke German, let alone Spanish) then he would translate into French for the locals.

'These boys they go catching this animals?' Jurgen said in his best English.

Jean-Francois asked the boys and they replied.

'This bush-pig,' Jean-Francois translated. 'He tasting very good. Yum-yum. For you one dollar.'

An idea was forming in Jurgen's mind.

'They catch him?'

'Yes,' came the eventual reply. They were experts at catching wild animals. Very, very good hunters.

'Tell them,' Jurgen said, drawing Jean-Francois to the side. 'They go catch me one chimpanzee. Bring him to Camp K.' He pointed to the cage containing the potto. 'Put him in cage like this.'

Jean-Francois explained. The boys all nodded eagerly. 'Pas de problème, chef,' one of them said, giving Jurgen two thumbs up.

'I give them ten dollars,' Jurgen added, and then explained about Ludger, the bamboo grove, the Mungu tree, the bananas and the nightly visits. Jurgen watched Jean-Francois relate the key details to the raggedy boys.

He was thinking: there was a small zoo in Victoireville, Douala's capital, a day's journey away. He could ship Ludger down to the zoo on one of the NGO convoys, his wounded leg could be examined and treated and he could spend the rest of his days in captivity, true, but in comfort and safety. He conjured up to himself an image of the label set on the bars of Ludger's capacious cage: "Ludger". Male Chimpanzee. Pan Troglodytes. Gift of Mr Jurgen Kiel. He would have done something good, Jurgen reckoned, pleased with himself, pleased with his initiative—his three months in Africa would have amounted to more than just guarding sacks of rice.

Three days later he was shaving in the wash-house when Severiano said that Jean-Francois was asking for him at the service-gate. Jurgen sauntered over to the small gate on the west side where the camp-workers came and went. Jean-Francois had been charged by Jurgen to purchase him 4000 American cigarettes on the Min'Jalli black market—twenty cartons of two-hundred cigarettes—the price was unbelievably low if you paid in American dollars. He was heading back home on leave in a week and he planned to hand out these cartons around Waldbach as Christmas gifts to his friends and acquaintances. Jean Francois was standing by the checkpoint with his hands in his pockets. He gestured him out with a covert twitch of his chin. No cigarettes, obviously, Jurgen reasoned, displeased. He followed Jean-Francois a few yards down the path. Three kids stood there with a wheelbarrow, a coloured cloth thrown over the contents.

'They get him for you,' Jean-Francois said with a knowing smile.

Jurgen knew at once but he felt he had to pull the cloth back just the same. Ludger lay there on his back, dead, blood from the big gash on his brow had trickled down to stain one side of his grey goatee. Apart from that he looked calm, Jurgen thought—his eyes closed, as if he were taking a lengthier than usual nap. Jurgen swore under his breath and felt a wave of strange emotion wash through him. He exhaled and looked up at the sky, veiled with a thin nacreous sheen of cloud. He looked down again and noticed that Ludger's stump was raw, alive with small beige maggots feeding. Ludger—lost in translation. Perhaps he'd done Ludger a favour—inadvertently saved him from a lingering gangrenous death... He would hold on to that thought—it would help.

'I wanted him alive,' Jurgen said emphatically, suddenly remembering the French word. 'Vivant.'

'You never say,' Jean-Francois replied. 'What you do with one big chimpanzee? You crazy man?'

One of the kids spoke.

'He say very good to eat. Good food,' Jean Francois

translated, rubbing his stomach. 'Yum-yum.'

'They can have him,' Jurgen said. 'I don't want to eat him.' He turned and began to walk back to the camp. Jean-Francois caught up with him, touched his elbow.

'Jurgen, mon ami, you owe these boys ten dollars.'

Jurgen paid.

The train to Waldbach from Straubing was cancelled, Jurgen saw from the noticeboard. The next one left in a couple of hours. Two hours in Straubing, Jurgen thought, wonderful, just what I was hoping for. His mood was bad because when he'd arrived in Munich he had telephoned his mother to let her know he was home from Africa. She said that she'd arranged for him to spend his leave at his sister's house. Ludger was going to be staying with her. 'It'll be easier,' his mother had said. 'You know how you and Ludger don't get on.' Jurgen deposited his kit bag in the left-luggage office and walked into Straubing. He didn't get on with Jochen, his sister's husband, either. A jazz musician, Jochen played the trombone in a casino nightclub. An annoying, opinionated man, he practised on his trombone two hours a day, seven days a week. It was a proud boast.

The handsome, wide main street of Straubing had been transformed into a Christmas market, full of small wooden huts selling food and drink and articles of woolly clothing. There was some sort of funfair also, Jurgen saw, strolling through the crowds, moving through successive aural zones of competing styles of music, and feeling a little self-conscious in his uniform, aware of the curious glances coming his way.

He went into a bar and had a few beers, trying to raise his mood, rebuking himself for his irritation and selfishness. His sister would make him very welcome, he knew, and he could easily go out for a walk when Jochen practised his trombone. Then a young girl—seventeen or eighteen—a bit drunk, he could tell, came and stood by the bar next to him to buy a drink. 'How many babies did you kill in Afghanistan?' she said, and then swore at him. Jurgen sighed, wished her a Happy Christmas, and left the bar.

'Welcome home,' he said to himself bitterly, standing by a wooden stall that was selling some kind of powerful and warming gluwein. Here the music was traditional, folksongs and Christmas carols that Jurgen could remember from his schooldays. He drank another couple of gluweins, feeling marginally better. The drink was strong, he saw, with some kind of aromatic schnapps in the mix. He flexed his shoulders, rolled his head: it was good to be back home, after all, one stupid drunk girl wasn't going to ruin his leave.

He saw that the traditional music was coming from an elaborate barrel organ, brightly painted, encrusted with carved wooden figurines from folk tales—witches and wizards, bears and foxes, lost boys and girls and gingerbread houses. He ordered another gluwein and wandered over with it to hear the music better. He dropped a couple of euros in the felt hat that dangled from the front. The man turning the handle of the barrel organ smiled and said thank you.

Then Jurgen saw the monkey sitting on the top. It was small and grey-furred but it had a white wisp of goatee on its chin, like Ludger, only miniature. There was a chain around its right leg attached to the barrel-organ. What kind of monkey was it? What were they called? A macaque? A gibbon? Jurgen whistled softly at it and it turned its head, its big round black eyes staring at Jurgen and it made a plaintive staccato cheeping sound and bared its sharp yellow teeth.

'What's this monkey called?' he asked the organ-grinder.

'Mo-Mo.'

'Mo-Mo? What kind of name is that?'

'You want a different name—get your own monkey.'

'OK,' Jurgen said, thinking. 'How much do you want for him?' Jurgen turned and smiled at the man.

'He's not for sale.'

'Everything's for sale,' Jurgen said. 'Just depends on the price. I'll give you a hundred euros.'

'He's not for sale, man,' the organist said, his faint smile fading. 'He's part of the act.'

'I'll give you two hundred euros.'

'Go and sober up somewhere, yeah? Leave me alone. Do me a favour.'

Jurgen emptied his pockets of money.

'Three hundred and twenty three euros,' Jurgen said, showing the man the money in his hands. 'You can buy six monkeys for that.'

'You buy six monkeys, you stupid, big moron—'

'I want this monkey. Only this monkey.'

'Why?'

'He reminds me of someone.'

'He's not for sale.' The organist stopped turning the handle. He came closer, and lowered his voice. 'If you don't stop bugging me, you cretin, I'll call the cops.'

For a second Jurgen thought about smashing the man in his self-satisfied face, of knocking him to the ground and kicking the shit out of him, but suddenly he had a better idea. He looked back at the little monkey, then back at the man.

'You think about that three hundred euros when you count your takings tonight. Asshole,' he said, and wandered off, casually.

The wire cutters cost eighteen euros. They had thick orange rubber handles and a capable-looking system of levers that quadrupled the pressure applied, so the assistant in the hardware store told him. Jurgen paid and walked back onto Straubing's main street.

He circled the organ player for a while, waiting for a few people to gather and claim his smiling attention. Then, with a couple of long strides, he came up swiftly behind the organ, grabbed the chain and cut it through, about three inches from the monkey's leg. It was like cutting string, it was so easy. The monkey turned and looked at him.

'Go, Mo-Mo,' Jurgen said softly. 'You're free.'

He stepped back and clapped his hands. And the monkey leapt off the organ and onto the roof of the next door shack that was selling alpaca hats and scarves.

'Hey!' the barrel-organist shouted. Jurgen darted off into the crowds of the funfair. He looked back. The monkey was sitting on the roof of the alpaca shack, and then suddenly it scurried along the looped electric cables attached to the wall of a nearby house and shimmied up a drainpipe to the guttering on the roof.

Jurgen felt a sense of ineffable happiness warm him, almost making his head reel. The last he saw of Mo-Mo was as he made his way daintily up the stepped-gable of the house to the rooftop. Then he climbed on to a television aerial and disappeared in the darkness. The whole of Straubing was out there, waiting for him, the whole of Bavaria, of Germany, Europe... Jurgen looked at his watch. Mo-Mo was free. He felt good. Time to catch the train to Waldbach.

A Duck in India

by Alice Newitt

(Alice Newitt aged 14 is the winner of a competition for children to write a story for *Just When Stories*).

It was approaching the last of the monsoon rains for that year; and the Indian plains were, for the Tapti family, saturated with prosperity.

The year had brought numerous windfalls, and they had used their errant profits to emigrate to Australia, primarily to indulge in their passion for koalas, opera and modern conveniences.

They had left their home, a basic shack, in the hands of an Egyptian relative who was spending the year in India on sabbatical leave. Before her arrival, the simple hut had been transformed.

It had become thoughtfully furnished, extravagantly styled and crammed with the rich Indian aromas of decadent spices and incenses; although mostly to disguise the failing roof and the rotting smell.

Had they known Rashida better, they wouldn't have made the effort, for she proved herself to be a very poor custodian indeed. The girl would spend her days lazing on the banks of the Ganges, immersed in the vibrancy and clatter, dreaming away to herself.

Meanwhile, the rains drove the undergrowth into the sanctuary of the hut, and the once lavish wallpapers became damaged and torn as malevolent locals stole in.

The resting animals in the roof watched the hut fall

A Duck in India

into disrepair, and gave forlorn quacks.

The river was lapping gently against its banks as Rashida drearily decided to spend that morning starting on her studies. Her intentions were noble, but the air was humid and soon she drifted off to sleep. She slept all day, until she was painfully awoken by a panicking cyclist riding over her legs. She was raw with sunburn, agitated by the bites covering her, and irritated by the low sun shining in her eyes. She supposed that the cyclist was mumbling apologies, but not knowing the local language she chose to misinterpret him.

The young man was rather alarmed when the young, attractive woman jumped on the back of his bicycle demanding a ride home. Nevertheless, he believed that it would be good entertainment to take her off-road, down the bumpy, pot-holed track through the wetlands. He was pleasantly surprised by her strong stomach, while she was unpleasantly shocked by his well-meaning, yet appalling skills as a cyclist.

He took her right up to the hut, accidently knocking over a few dead pot plants on the veranda in the process. She thanked him wearily as he reattached a wheel that was falling off and went into the shady recluse of the hut.

Bending down under the table, she frantically rummaged through the assortment of papers, clothes and fruit left there, looking for something that might treat insect bites. She was wondering whether a rotting mango might do the job when to her dismay, but not to her surprise, she found a nesting snake. A little annoyed that it had been making a mess on her favourite tablecloth, she wrapped it up and threw it out of the window.

It was then that she noticed, for the first time, that perhaps she ought to sort the place out as, after all, it wasn't her home to wreck. A few weeks before, a surge of creativity had come over her and she had purchased three tins of emulsion (deep magenta, stardust gold and baby pink), several rolls of elaborate wallpaper and an assortment of wall hangings and rugs. She had also dug out a sculpture that she'd won in a raffle a long time ago, along with a rather large vase that came free with her bulk order of rice. It was time, she declared, to put them to use.

Roping in the assistance of Milind, the man with the bicycle, Rashida spent the evening transforming the hut into a vivid, glowing creation to rival the amber sunset outside.

Milind took all the exotic creatures back to the Gangentic plains where they belonged, and laughed when a family of ducks kept following him back, diving under Rashida's coffee table.

The lantern light casted a orange glow in the dark landscape, while Rashida and Milind lay back on the veranda, listening to the whistles and clicks, and the distant hums of the city.

Just as Rashida began to doze off, her eyes heavy from squinting at the glistening stars above, she felt something nuzzling her palm. She sat up, curious, and saw an elegant duck trying to eat the grasses growing through the strips of wood.

Its bottom half was a thousand shades of brown, but its head and neck ware baby pink. It struck Rashida that the duck had been mucking up her delicate paintwork, and she shooed it away angrily. Milind cried out urgently.

'What?' shouted Rashida in a strained attempt at Hindi.

'It's a pink headed duck! They're meant to be extinct!' explained Milind.

'Stop shouting!'

'Very very rare!'

'What?'

As Rashida and Milind argued in their dysfunctional way, the duck slipped away into the darkness of the sandy street, out of the light of the hut.

The duck was desperate for food. Lost in the hut for days, it hadn't been able to find much to eat, and the candlelight had confused it. Nocturnal, the noise during the day had disturbed its sleeping habits, and the hissing snake had made it wary.

Quacking quietly, the duck waddled aimlessly in zigzags across the road, lost and bewildered. It passed a couple on a late evening stroll.

'Look at this, Kate!' said the towering British man, pointing. 'It's half duck, half flamingo!'

'It's cute!' said the lady, entwined in the man's arm, smiling down.

'It's weird!' jeered the man.

'Don't be mean,' scolded the lady, bending down to pat the duck. 'Take a picture, Dave.'

The duck dived away as Kate's hand came close. The camera flashed, capturing only Kate's outstretched hand.

The creature didn't belong on land; its home was the wetlands. It needed to get back with a flock, any flock. The solo life was a threat to its survival, even more so than fiery women or naïve tourists.

Plodding on, the duck passed many silent, dark houses with gated driveways. It passed bright houses, with music blaring and party guests falling out of them. It passed sheds filled to the brim with worldly possessions. It passed holiday lets, with swimming pools and barbeques. It passed shops, with vegetables next to laundry baskets, carpets next to newspapers.

The world span around the duck, but gradually the houses became less frequent and the ground grew wet and squidgy beneath its feet. It was approaching the wetlands, and getting nearer to a flock.

All of a sudden, the duck felt the ground shaking, and there was a low rumbling. Glaring headlights lit the dirt track. The duck darted off the road just in time, as the van screeched to a halt. A man leapt out of the truck, and grabbed the duck. It struggled helplessly. They were discussing it in Hindi, about how it would look nice in their windowsill, get the profits up, fetch a good price.

Just as they were stuffing it into the van, Milind crashed into the vehicle. He fell into a heap on the floor, causing one of the men to lose his grip on the pink headed duck, and it broke free.

Milind had been pedaling everywhere, trying to track the duck so that he could take it to the wetlands. Rashida had been running not far behind him. They had almost given up hope, but after a lot of arm-flapping trying to ask after the duck, a British couple had managed to understand them and pointed them in the right direction.

Frantic, Milind had ridden as fast as he could, but pot hole after pot hole had caused him to lose control. The men with the van were not impressed with Milind, but he and Rashida didn't stay to listen.

Leaving the bike in the road, which the men took in place of the duck, Milind and Rashida ran through the undergrowth, listening out for the quacks and whistles

Alice Newitt

of the duck.

They found it, nesting under a leafy bush, with deep magenta coloured berries. Milind picked it up gently, and they trekked to the edge of the wetland to set it free.

When they reached the marshland, the duck quickly waddled away, quacking, searching. He disappeared into the reeds as the stardust gold halo of the sun could be seen setting behind the dark silhouette of the city.

Rashida and Milind stood close together, listening to croaks, tweets, chatter, clicks and one more noise that could defy any language barrier.

The lonely quack of the last of the pink headed ducks.

Zushkaali and the Elephant

by Angela Young

Of all the creatures in all the world, the elephants are the most like us. They can be sad like us, they can be frightened like us, they can be happy like us and, like us, they can be angry. Elephants who are left alone for too long are never happy elephants. They like being with their fellow elephants. Just like us.

But it was not always so.

A long, long time ago the elephants who lived in the heart of the heart of Africa were, well, just elephants, and not at all like us.

And it was in those times that, one very hot day, a strong young bull elephant was so busy eating delicious shoots and leaves that he didn't notice his fellow elephants moving on. When he stopped eating and looked up, they were gone. The elephant found himself all by himself for the first time in his life, and strange things began happening to him. His eyes filled with water and a lump grew in his throat. His skin tingled and his knees went weak. He lifted his trunk to bellow for his fellow elephants, but the lump in his throat was so large that his bellow got stuck behind it. Only a soft sad bleat found its way past the lump and it wasn't loud enough to summon his fellow elephants.

It was then that the earth heard the soft sad bleat deep

down in her heart and, because it was the saddest sound she'd ever heard, she decided to do everything in her power to help the elephant. First of all she cried some large tears from her clouds because she felt so sorry for the elephant—and her tears cooled him down—and then the earth spoke to the elephant.

'Don't be sad, oh please don't be sad.' She said, 'I'll give you all the powers you need to help you find your fellow elephants. You'll soon see them again. I promise.'

The water stopped spilling from the elephant's eyes and his knees felt stronger. He felt cooler from the rain and, while he listened to the earth, he felt his heart fluttering and jumping.

'I will give you the leaping and the running power,' said the earth, 'and I will give you the flying power. The swimming power will soon be yours and so will the curling and coiling and twisting and bending powers. I will give you the power of excellent eyesight and the power to make yourself as small as possible, just in case.'

And so it was that, with these unaccustomed powers, the elephant leapt and ran and flew and swam all over the earth looking for his fellow elephants. He picked up small creatures in his tusks that curled and coiled and twisted and bent, and he asked the small creatures if they'd seen his fellow elephants. At night he made himself as small as possible so that he could sleep in tiny rock caves and not feel so alone. But the elephant did not find his fellow elephants because elephants do not live in the air, nor do they live in rivers or lakes, nor in tiny rock caves. And the elephant's fellows never saw him because they were not looking for a leaping elephant or a flying elephant or even a swimming elephant. Nor were they looking for an elephant with tusks that curled and coiled and twisted and bent. Or an elephant who could make himself as small as could be. And even if they had been looking for such an elephant, their eyesight was so poor that they would have missed him.

So the earth, who had truly meant to help the elephant, had not helped him at all.

And so it was that, on a day when the elephant was flying over a red desert in the heart of the heart of Africa, he saw five creatures in a huddle on the ground. He was so pleased to find other creatures because he had been by himself for so long that he flew down straight away, and his heart fluttered and jumped.

'I'm looking for my fellow elephants,' he said in his soft sad bleat, 'have you seen them?'

'No,' snarled the lion.

'No,' cawed the eagle.

'No,' hissed the fish.

Zushkaali and the Elephant

'No,' spat the snake.

And the huge hyrax* just looked at the elephant and did not say a word.

The lion curled his lips up over his teeth and said: 'We'd only see your fellow elephants if they came right up to us, right here in the red desert. We can't go anywhere because you have the powers that are rightfully ours. I can't leap or run.'

'And I can't fly, or see properly.'

'I can't swim.'

'And I can't curl or coil or twist or bend.'

And the huge hyrax just looked at the elephant and did not say a word.

The elephant felt hot all over and he bellowed. And his bellow blasted past the lump in his throat, and he stamped his feet and the earth shuddered.

'This is very wrong,' bellowed the elephant. 'The earth has given me powers that were never meant for me, powers that are rightfully yours.'

The elephant stamped his feet heavily on the dry earth and his huge ears flapped backwards and forwards and then he charged. And as the elephant charged across

---

* Small ungulate mammal of Africa and Asia with rodent-like teeth and feet with hoof-like toes. The closest living relative to the Elephant!.

the red desert he bellowed to the earth: 'Give these creatures back their rightful powers this minute! THIS MINUTE!'

But the earth, even though she was frightened of the elephant, remained silent. She had fallen in love with the young bull elephant and so she wanted him to have all the powers. She would not help the other creatures.

After a while the elephant stopped bellowing and he stopped charging, and then he felt the lump in his throat once more. He looked helplessly at the creatures and his skin tingled and water flowed from his eyes and his knees went weak. The elephant's tired body collapsed onto the earth. He didn't know what to do.

But the creatures, who thought the elephant was just putting on a show and didn't really want to give them back their rightful powers, suddenly and heartlessly attacked him.

'If you won't give us back our rightful powers,' snarled the lion who could not leap or run, 'we'll just take them,' and he tore into the elephant's legs.

'Rightfully ours, rightfully ours,' cawed the eagle who could not fly and could not see properly. And he made a blind lunge for one of the elephant's ears with his sharp pointed beak.

The elephant's skin tingled and his knees went so weak that he was glad he wasn't standing up.

Zushkaali and the Elephant

'They're not yours, they're not yours,' hissed the fish who could not swim, and she scratched her prickly scales up and down the elephant's body.

'Kill him, kill him and then the powers will be rightfully ours,' spat out the snake who could not curl or coil or twist or bend.

The heartless creatures tore at the elephant until they were exhausted, but still the lion could not leap or run and the eagle could not fly or see properly. The fish still could not swim and the snake could not curl or coil or twist or bend.

Only the huge hyrax did not attack the elephant. He just turned his head away and did not say a word.

'I think the elephant is dying,' spat the snake who could not curl or coil or twist or bend, 'and still he has the powers that are rightfully ours.'

And then a deep voice boomed out across the red desert. 'The powers cannot be taken,' said the voice, 'they can only be given.'

The deep voice was Zushkaali's voice, the wise man of those times. He spoke as he strode towards the creatures. His long striped tunic billowed on the wind and the sash of his striped turban streamed out behind him.

The creatures hung their heads because they knew that Zushkaali the Wise always spoke the truth, and they knew he was angry with them.

'From the day the earth gave the elephant all the powers,' said Zushkaali, 'they have been his to use as he will. And if he so wishes, he can give the powers away, but they cannot be taken from him.'

The elephant heard Zushkaali's deep strong voice and his soft sad bleat squeezed past the lump in his throat. Now he knew just what to do. 'I would like to give each of you,' he said, lifting his head and setting his jaws down squarely on the ground, 'the powers that are rightfully yours.'

The elephant's jaws rattled on the dry ground and the lump, which was now brittle and hard, rattled in the back of his throat when he spoke.

The elephant looked first at the lame lion who hung his head because he was ashamed of what he'd done to the elephant. 'I give you the leaping and the running power,' rattled out the elephant, 'for these are the powers that are rightfully yours.'

The lame lion felt his legs filling up with the leaping and the running power and the elephant's legs collapsed and grew weak. The lame lion's legs grew stronger and stronger until, with one powerful bound, he leapt over the elephant's body and away into the red desert.

'Now you, earthbound, almost blind eagle,' said the elephant in his voice with the rattle in it.

Zushkaali and the Elephant

The eagle who could not fly stood awkwardly, trying to balance the weight of his useless wings. He too hung his head and, at that moment, he was glad he could not see properly.

'I give you the flying power and the power of excellent eyesight,' said the elephant. 'For those are the powers that are rightfully yours.'

The earthbound eagle felt his wings filling up with the flying power and when he spread his wings and flapped them a little, he soared effortlessly into the air, while the elephant's wing-ears collapsed and shrank and he felt the flying power drain out of them. And when the eagle looked down as he flew over the red desert he found that his eyesight was so restored that he could distinguish grains of sand one from the other, while the elephant's vision grew cloudy and short-sighted and he closed his eyes.

The fish who could not swim came next, but she could not look at the dying elephant either. Instead she simply scratched her scales across the sand and, when she reached the elephant, she stayed very still by his side.

'I give you the swimming power,' said the elephant, his voice now loud with the rattles and his eyes still closed, 'for that is the power that is rightfully yours.' The fish who lived on dry land scraped her way to the river bank and when she reached the river, the swimming power had so filled her body that she swam strongly and well. By the time the sun rose the next day she was swimming in the sea.

The elephant's voice rattled on and the stiff awkward snake hauled herself up onto the elephant's trunk and heaved herself awkwardly through the curls and the coils and the twists and the bends of the elephant's great white tusks.

'I give you the curling and the coiling, the twisting and the bending powers,' rattled out the elephant, 'for these are the powers that are rightfully yours.' The stiff awkward snake felt the powers surge into her stiff awkward body and then she curled and coiled and twisted and bent her way across the red desert, while the elephant's tusks hardened and straightened themselves along the red sand on either side of his mouth. All these things the elephant sensed rather than saw, because his eyesight was by now so poor.

And at last the huge hyrax who had not said a word stood right in front of the elephant. He was as tall as the elephant's head and all he wanted was to be as small as possible. The elephant's voice was wracked with rattles but when he felt the huge hyrax's breath on his trunk he managed to say, 'You did not attack me... and that makes you a brother.' And then after a long pause he said, 'Say after me: I want to be small, as small as can be,' and here the elephant's rattling voice failed him.

The huge hyrax opened and shut his mouth, but because he could not say a word, not a word came out. Just then the elephant coughed and the brittle lump at the back of his throat flew out of his mouth. At exactly the same time the huge hyrax breathed in and he felt something vibrating wildly against the back of his throat. He almost choked, then he coughed and his cough had a rattle in it, and then he spoke, and his voice was the elephant's voice, the voice with a rattle in it.

'I want to be small, as small as can be.'

The huge hyrax was thrilled with his new rattling voice. He so liked the sound of it that he added some words of his own; and each time he rattled out the words he shrank a size, and when he was very small he ran up the elephant's trunk and kissed the elephant on his forehead.

'Thank you,' said the very small hyrax in his rattling voice, 'thank you.'

'Thank YOU,' said the elephant, 'for not ... ', and then he stopped because his voice wasn't rattling and the brittle lump was gone. He started again. 'Thank you for not attacking me and for taking away the rattle and the lump.' The very small hyrax gave the elephant another kiss and then he scuttled down the elephant's trunk and away into the red desert. The elephant's heart fluttered and jumped as he listened until even he, whose hearing had always been good, could no longer hear the very small hyrax.

The earth's heart was fluttering and jumping too. She wanted to speak to the elephant, but her voice was choked with tears so her clouds burst open and poured out their rain on the elephant whose blood had spilled all around him on the earth. Night fell and the elephant slept and while he was sleeping Zushkaali the Wise knelt beside him. He soothed the elephant with his hands and with his voice, but he saw that the elephant's wounds were grave, so he summoned the spiders.

'Come quickly,' he said, 'come very quickly.'

The spiders crawled out from under stones all across the red desert and when they reached the elephant they began to spin their healing webs. The spiders hummed a healing hum as they spun out their healing webs, and the earth rained down her tears.

Zushkaali the Wise sat by the elephant until the earth dried her tears and the sun made the raindrops sparkle on the spiders' healing webs which, by then, covered all the elephant's wounds.

'I am so sorry,' said the earth. Her voice was crystal clear after the rain, 'I loved you so much that I wanted you to have everything, all the powers, everything that I could give you. I never meant to do you any harm.'

Zushkaali and the Elephant

'I know,' said the elephant in a new strong voice. 'I know that you meant well.' The elephant kissed the earth. 'Anyone could have made the same mistake,' he said and the earth's heart fluttered and jumped and the elephant's heart fluttered and jumped and then the elephant stood up. The spiders' healing webs clung to his body.

Zushkaali the Wise led the elephant to a newly filled watering hole. As he walked, the elephant trod carefully to avoid squashing any sleeping spiders. When he reached the watering hole the elephant took a long drink and then he looked into Zushkaali's wide green eyes.

'Strange things have happened to me since I lost my fellow elephants,' he said. 'First the earth gave me powers that were not rightfully mine,' the elephant looked at Zushkaali, 'and I gave them back. But a lump grew in my throat and water spilled from my eyes. My skin tingled and my knees went weak. My heart has been fluttering and jumping up and down and I got hot all over and I bellowed and I charged and I stamped my feet. What are these things, Zushkaali?' said the elephant. 'What has been happening to me?'

'What's been happening to you,' said Zushkaali, 'is what the human creatures call feelings. Feelings have been happening to you.'

'What are feelings?' said the elephant.

'I'll tell you as we travel,' said Zushkaali the Wise, and so the elephant knelt down and Zushkaali climbed onto his back just behind his huge ears that had, until so very recently, been his wings.

They travelled together across the red desert and as the sash from Zushkaali's turban billowed out behind them like a flag, and the spiders' healing webs fell away when they'd done their healing work, Zushkaali told the elephant everything he wanted to know.

'The feeling that comes when your eyes spill over with water and a lump grows in your throat,' said Zushkaali, 'is called sadness. Sadness comes if you are by yourself for too long, or if someone you love dies. The water that spilled from your eyes are called tears. And just before the tears come a lump grows in your throat that makes it difficult to speak.'

'Sadness,' repeated the elephant. 'Tears.' And he remembered what happened when he looked up and saw that his fellow elephants weren't there any more.

'The feeling that comes when your skin tingles and your knees feel weak is called fear,' said Zushkaali.

'Fear,' repeated the elephant, and he remembered what happened when the creatures attacked him.

'Fear comes when you're worried that you might be hurt, or when you don't feel very safe,' said Zushkaali.

They travelled on in silence for a while until

Zushkaali and the Elephant

Zushkaali said, 'And the feeling that comes when your heart flutters and jumps up and down is called happiness. Some call it joy.'

'Happiness,' repeated the elephant, 'joy.' And he remembered all the times that his heart had fluttered and jumped and particularly he remembered how it had fluttered and jumped when the hyrax had kissed him.

'Happiness and joy come for many reasons,' said Zushkaali, 'but they are especially near when you are close to the creatures you love, when you are close to your fellow creatures. And last but not least,' said Zushkaali, 'the feeling that comes when you get hot all over and bellow and charge and stamp your feet is called anger. Anger often comes when somebody does something that is wrong.'

'Anger,' repeated the elephant, and he remembered what had happened when he realised that the earth had given him the powers that were not rightfully his.

Zushkaali and the elephant travelled on in silence, and this time the silence lasted for a long time. And then, at last, the elephant asked Zushkaali about a word that he'd been wondering about ever since he'd heard Zushkaali say it.

'What is love?' said the elephant. But just as the elephant asked that question he heard and smelled his fellow elephants ahead. He heard them slooshing water all over each other and he knew by the smell that they were at their favourite watering hole. He heard them trumpeting. And then the elephant's heart turned a somersault and he longed to curl his trunk around his fellow elephants and rub himself up against them. He walked faster.

'The feeling that you are feeling now is called love,' said Zushkaali.

The elephant walked faster and faster and Zushkaali the Wise held onto the elephant's ears with both hands so that he wouldn't fall off. The elephant ran as fast as elephants can towards his fellow elephants.

'And to feel all these feelings,' said Zushkaali, bouncing up and down behind the elephant's ears and laughing, 'and to know what they are called is the power that is rightfully yours.'

When, at last, the elephant was reunited with his fellow elephants he showed them just how he felt about them. When they understood what he was showing them, they showed him that they felt the same love for him, the same sadness when he was not with them, the same fear when they didn't know where to find him, the same happiness and the same joy when they saw him coming back, and the same anger with the earth for giving him the powers that were not rightfully his so that they wouldn't recognise him even if they had seen him.

The young bull elephant told his fellow elephants

Zushkaali and the Elephant

the names of all these feelings, so they now understood that, like the lion and the eagle, like the fish and the snake, and like the smallest little hyrax with his voice with the rattle in it, they all possessed the powers that were rightfully theirs.

'And the rightful powers for an elephant,' said the elephant, 'are the feeling powers.'

And since that time so very long ago in the heart of the heart of Africa, every elephant has felt these feelings, and that is why they, of all the creatures, are the most like us, the human creatures.

And the Dolphin Smiled

by Jin Pyn Lee

Once, where the river met the ocean full of yellow, red, orange and blue, there lived a dolphin and a boy.

Everyday the dolphin and the boy would play.

They would tell each other stories of the world as they saw it in their own ways.

'This is a place', the dolphin would say, 'where bubbles always leave a trace, and fish swim in schools with grace. A place, may I add, where giant catfish play catch, not fetch, where mussels play hide so that no one can seek. A place filled with swishes, pops, tunes, and clicks. A home in which my brothers, sisters, mum and I, frolic.'

But of colours the dolphin could not speak, for her eyes could not see the light of day. You see, dolphins of the rivers can only hear.

The young boy, on the other hand, could listen, touch, smell and see. He would tell his dolphin friend about his world of colours he sees so freely.

'This is a place,' the boy would praise, 'where the land is green, and the sky is blue, whilst in-betweens are filled with other amazing hues, such as the pink and grey you have on you.'

'But the best sight of all, is you my friend, and that smile on your face.'

And that, to the dolphin, was the best sound of all.

And the Dolphin Smiled

When it was time to fish, where the river met the ocean full of purple, green, gold and other shimmering hues, the boy would softly row his small wooden boat whilst the dolphin would spit and splash, till the fish were caught.

'Spit, splash, spit, splash. We work the fish into the net.'

'Spit, splash, spit, splash. And then we release most of our catch.'

The two would have so much fun working together.

So the boy and the dolphin were full, and happy.

Days passed. Then months. And years.

Every day the dolphin would wait for the boy. His light footsteps a sweet rhythm to her ears. And every day the boy would look out for the dolphin's sweet smile bobbing out from the water of the river that met the ocean full of pink, grey and wonderful blues.

One day the boy said, 'This boat is too small for me.'

And he went and bought a big boat.

'Grrrr! Wrrrr!' The boat was loud. But the boy could not hear.

The dolphin was scared. She could not see and now even her hearing was fading.

Still the dolphin smiled. She gave her friend her brightest smile.

But the boy could no longer see.

'I'm still hungry,' the boy said, after he had caught all

the fish with his fancy new boat.

So off he went, and built factories. Factories that smeared the blue sky and the river that met the ocean, full of yellow, orange, red and blue, with a foul-smelling black.

There were no more colours.

Still, the dolphin smiled.

But the boy who could no longer see and no longer smell, was still hungry.

So he went and built a dam.

And when that happened, there was silence.

No one came, and no one went. No mussels, no bubbles, no fish. No food. There were no more sounds. No swishes, pops, tunes and clicks.

One by one, the dolphin's brothers, sisters, and mother, fell to the bottom of the river.

Yet, still, the dolphin with tears in her eyes that could not see the light of day, smiled at the boy.

And the boy, still hungry, took the smile, the last of her kind, to an aquarium where all of his kind could touch and see, for a fee.

Days passed, then months.

As the dolphin lay at the bottom of the tank of no colour and no sound, she heard familiar footsteps. Though no longer light, they were still sweet rhythm to her ears. Then she heard a familiar voice.

And the Dolphin Smiled

'I too have now lost my sight, and now I can hardly hear, much less smell. But here in front of you, my dear son,' said the boy who was now an old man, to his boy, 'is the best sight of all.'

As he spoke a wondrous thing happened. Colour flooded the dolphin's eyes. In her sight, the dolphin, and now the old man's boy could see the blue sky, green land, and the river that meets the ocean full of yellow, red, orange, and all the world's shimmering hues.

And the dolphin smiled.

George the Tortoise

by Antonia Michaelis

Thomas Harlow's first thought was: My God, that's an ugly animal. He didn't know if God existed, but he was certain that this giant tortoise was the ugliest he had ever seen. But it was the last of its kind. That was why Thomas was there at Santa Cruz, thousand of miles far away from home, a few air miles to Ecuador and many sea miles from Ecuador to the Galapagos islands.

'George', he said to the tortoise. 'Hello, George.'

It was hot. He was nervous.

'Are you nervous?' the woman next to him asked.

He forced a smile.

'It's hot,' he said.

She nodded.

'We are near the equator. The sun is almost vertically above us. George is lucky with his shell. It's as if he was born with a big hat to protect him against the sun.'

She laughed.

She was young, almost childlike. Her hair was dark and her eyes darker. He asked himself why such a beautiful woman would want to spend her life with an ugly tortoise.

'Do you see the curve at the front of his shell?' she asked, 'the saddle, as we say. It is unique. There are many different tortoises but this one is an Abingdonii. There is only one left...'

He nodded. He knew all this. She had written to him several times. 'Nobody knows how old he is,' she said. 'Something between 50 and 80. I would be nervous speaking to such a rare creature. I am so curious about what he is going to tell you...what he likes...tell him that we are going to do everything...' She pressed her slim hands together, opened her mouth as if she wanted to add something, closed it again and walked off on one of the tidy paths at the Charles Darwin Research Centre. She left him alone.

He was alone with the world's ugliest tortoise, a burning equatorial sun and an impossible mission. She had thought he was nervous because he didn't know what George would tell him. But she was wrong. He was nervous because he was frightened she would find out that he was a fraud. George would not tell him anything. She had invited him to come because she had found his website. Now, he cursed his website.

Dr. Thomas Harlow, animal psychologist, it said on his webpage in a blue font with a purple background. 'Do you have a problem with your loved one? I can offer an unusual solution. I can talk to your pets. After years of meditation and exercises I have learned to talk to animals.

'I tune myself into their wavelength and receive the signals of their thoughts. This is the best method to establish the needs of your dog or cat, and for more difficult animals I can offer psychoanalysis. Often the difficulties are hidden in the past. Choose the path that many others have chosen before you. Get in touch with Dr Thomas Harlow.'

He had sat in front of many dogs and cats and had looked them straight in the eye. For hours. For days. For years. And he had never ever heard a single word, or felt a thing. The truth was, he disliked dogs and cats. He disliked all animals. If he was honest with himself, he didn't particularly like humans either. He certainly didn't feel guilty about cheating on them. But his PhD was real. He had a PhD in botany. He didn't believe in psychoanalysis. He did not believe in signals. He believed in the money that he earned.

It was good money. Pet owners were happy when someone told them their cat needed a cat tree, or that their dog bit the postman because as a puppy an evil postman kicked him. But this was different. This was a big thing. For years, scientists from all over the world had tried to encourage George, the last example of the Abingdonii Tortoise, to mate and reproduce. Reproduce, at least, with similar tortoises. But George had refused. When he died his species would be extinct. And humans would feel guilty.

'Talking to animals,' said a voice behind him.

George the Tortoise

'That's something you can do? You tune into the right wavelength. You understand the signals of their thoughts. What else? Do you fly as well if the wind has the right wavelength?'

'No.' He sighed. 'You are welcome to poke fun at me,' said Thomas. 'But leave me in peace now while I give it a try.'

The person behind him giggled. No. The giggling did not come from behind him. It came from in front of him.

'Idiot,' said the voice. 'Signals. Wavelengths. Psychoanalysis. Ha!'

Thomas blinked. There was nobody in front of him. Only George. George stood on his huge ugly legs near the pond, stretched his wrinkly neck and looked at him with his small eyes. 'I know what you are thinking,' said the voice.

'You are thinking: ugly.'

Thomas twitched. 'George?' he asked silently.

'It's Jorge actually, but you can call me George,' the voice said. It was the voice of an old man—the kind of old man you see in hospitals complaining about the food.

'I am still Ecuadorian even if most researchers speak English.'

'You...you are speaking...to me? Here, now? In...my language?'

'I have had enough time to learn English. There is not much to do around here.'

Thomas shook his head. 'I can do it... I can really do it!' he stammered. 'All this magic with the dogs and cats...and I didn't know that I can really do it! That's impossible. I can really talk to animals!'

'Nonsense,' said George. 'You can't do anything. I talk to humans. Sit down again. It's impossible to have a conversation with you up there.'

Thomas realised that he had jumped up. He sat down again on the stone wall surrounding the turtle enclosure. His knees were shaking.

'How do you know what my website says?'

George laughed. It was the hoarse laughter of an old man. The wrinkles on his neck trembled. 'What if I tell you that I have internet access as well? The connection is sometimes bad but usually I get all the information I need.' He laughed even more when he saw Thomas's face. He shook his wrinkly neck and roared with laughter.

'You didn't believe that, did you?' he giggled.

'You don't have access to the internet, do you?'

'My God, I am a tortoise, not a human. Camilla told me about it. The human being with the beautiful eyes who was here a short while ago. The one who got you here.'

'If you can talk to the humans...why don't you speak

George the Tortoise

to Camilla?'

'Imagine if I would speak to the people in the centre. What a to-do there would be! It's more than enough that I am the last of my species.'

Thomas shook his head and tried to think clearly.

'Ok,' he said. 'Let's talk. They want you to reproduce, so that your species doesn't become extinct. They want to ask you what's wrong. I mean there are two lovely female tortoises in the enclosure...'

The females were busy eating leaves. They were a bit smaller than George but otherwise looked the same as him.

'I could tell you a secret', whispered George.

'Anything to do with those two over there?'

'With them? No. It is a really, really big secret.' He winked conspiratorially and moved closer on his clumsy feet.

'My secret begins in the past. It is an old secret from way back when I was born. Well actually, I was laid, as an egg, on a beach not far from here. On Pinta island.

'Back then everything was different, of course. Pinta Island was covered with rain forest. Sunflower trees opened their umbrella-like blossoms over the dense jungle of cat's claw and ferns. Mistletoe and orchids climbed over branches and in the humid air thousands of birds sang, animals rustled, insects flew...and further down, the butterfly bush with its white blossoms and heavy branches, swayed in the wind. As for the beach, ahh yes, the beach was filled with the fragrance of the passionflower; its flowers so complicated...and Darwin's cotton shining in yellow lampions. But on the rocky coast where only the whisker cactus grew, there I was hidden in a cave.

'I hatched on a Monday. Of course, I could not have known that it was a Monday but it felt like a Monday. Like a beginning.

'The shell of the egg burst. I waited for a while to see if anything would happen. Nothing happened. The only thing I heard was the cracking of another eggshell. I started to dig upwards to leave the cave. Another tortoise dug alongside me. Perhaps there were more tortoises behind us, I don't know. But at some stage the sunlight was shining into my eyes and I saw her. She was very pretty with her oval shell and her four slim legs.

"Hello," I said. "Do you want to discover what it is, this world?"

'The other tortoise didn't say anything. She seemed a little shy. But when I started walking she followed me. We left the shrubs and reached the rocky beach and then we saw the sea. It was so blue and so big and so endless.

"Let's have a closer look," I said.

"But we are land tortoises," she said.

George the Tortoise

"Only a look," I said.

'In this moment a shadow approached over the rocks. And we lifted our heads. Above us flew a buzzard. I knew that it was a buzzard and that it meant certain death. I knew that I had to do something, something special, something tortoises do—but I didn't know what.

'I looked at the endless blue sea.

"Dive." I said.

"We are land tortoises," she said.

'But I had started running. I ran as fast as I could towards the blue. With a last final leap I reached it. The blue water felt cool and new. I was frightened of the deep and of...infinity. But my legs knew how to swim. When I surfaced and looked back, I saw the buzzard again, up in the air. He was carrying something in his talons. The tortoise that had hatched next to me, was nowhere to be seen on the beach.

'When I climbed back on land I was very, very sad. Only a few minutes in this world and I already knew about laughter and infinity, about death and sadness. These were all big things for a small tortoise. Without this other tortoise, my life seemed to make no sense.

'I gave a name to the other tortoise. I called her Sentida, a Spanish word meaning Heartfelt.

'In time I grew and grew. Bigger and bigger and bigger... I am a Galapagos giant tortoise, the largest living tortoise...an Abingdonii. Back then there were many of us. I ate leaves and drank dew and when no other tortoise was looking I swam in the infinite sea.

'When I was a grown up and could reach the blossoms of the yellow cotton, a Monday came again. The feeling that it is Monday, I mean. A feeling of a fresh start. Like a colour that one can only smell with one's big toe, if one breathes very quietly. I was six years old and far from being an adult. I moved my head gently into my shell to think about things—when suddenly someone cleared their throat.

"Hello," said the voice, which sounded familiar. "Excuse me...are you the tortoise who said DIVE?"

"Dive?" I asked and appeared from my shell.

'And if I weren't a tortoise I would have fallen over in astonishment. In front of me was HER. Sentida.

"You are...but...the buzzard!" I stuttered.

'Sentida sighed. "I am one of the few tortoises that ever flew. I dived, back inside my shell."

"That was it!" I exclaimed. "That was what one had to do!"

"The buzzard realised that he couldn't eat me and then dropped me on the other side of the island," said Sentida.

"I ran into the sea thinking that I might be able to swim. Therefore I swam. When I returned to the land the Buzzard had gone."

George the Tortoise

"What a surprise to bump into each other again!" I exclaimed. "After all these years!"

"Coincidence, well..." said Sentida and look down on her toes. "I... I am not very good at finding things again. That's how women are. It took me years to return here to find you."

I learned a new thing that Monday. I discovered happiness. Unlike a buzzard it has no talons.' George fell silent. 'No talons,' he repeated after a while.

'And the secret?' asked Thomas. 'You wanted to tell me about a secret.'

'Secret?' The eyes of the old tortoise were still looking into the past.

'Yes. It's about a treasure. A treasure everyone is looking for. But I am tired. Return tomorrow. Then I will tell you about the treasure.'

'I will not be able to sleep,' Thomas said. 'I will think about the treasure all night long. Tell me one last thing. The ladies over there? Why do you not...'

The female tortoises were still eating their leaves. 'Their lives seem to depend on leaves,' George snorted. 'They are not from my kind.'

'But they are closely related to your kind.'

'Would a human kiss an orang-utan?'

Thomas thought for a moment. 'That depends,' Thomas laughed.

'Depends on how much he's drunk before.'

'Who, the human or the orang utan?'

'We can see each other tomorrow,' he said. George nodded with his wrinkly neck. He did not seem so ugly anymore. Only very old. 'Say hello to Camilla,' he said. 'The human with the beautiful dark eyes.'

Camilla sat on a wall at the entrance of the centre. She was nervously chewing her nails. When she saw Thomas she jumped up.

'What did he say? Why doesn't he want to have children?'

Thomas shook his head. 'We are not there yet,' he replied. 'Psychology is a complicated thing. I believe that the problem lies in his childhood. We have just reached the point when he is six years old.'

Then he strolled away towards the coast in search of a place where he could steal a view of Pinta Island. He might possibly have to walk to the other end of Santa Cruz. He hoped it would not take him six years.

* * *

'So. Did you have a rest?' asked Thomas.

'Yes thank you, it was alright,' replied George. 'At my age I don't sleep well anymore. Mostly I just close my eyes and look into the past. I can choose what part of the

George the Tortoise

past I want to live in. It all depends on my mood.'

He observed Thomas with his sparkling eyes. 'But you are young and impatient. You want to hear about the treasure. It is valuable, very valuable. To be precise, it has a value of ten thousand dollars.' Thomas whistled through his teeth. Ten thousand dollars, he thought, would come in very handy.

'At around six years old a tortoise is learning what to eat, how to forecast the weather, how to withdraw into its shell and how to live in its own imagination and memories. Sentida and I learned these things together. We spent every day together except those times when she got lost. She never learned how to find her way back to me so it was my job to find her. We spent ten years learning together. Life was peaceful. Then one day the goats arrived, brought here by humans. The first pair of goats were a bit stupid but did not upset anyone. But this pair of goats created a young one. And when they grew, they gave birth to other young ones. Suddenly there were more and more goats. Every now and then the humans came and killed some goats to eat. But they could never eat them all.

'The goats however ate everything. They ate the tender grass in the glades, the yellow leaves of the cotton. Then they ate the white passionflowers and the silver bark of the torchwood trees. Then the cafetillo bush. Finally, they ate the jungle. They climbed the trees on their hooves and they ate and ate. Nothing was left for us. It wasn't the fault of the goats. They were trapped on the island. They weren't buzzards, they couldn't fly away. They had to eat what they could find.

'Then rats arrived on the island as well. They must have come with the boats. The rats ate our eggs. Sentida and I walked long distances to find just a few yellow blossoms of the cotton plant. We walked miles to find food. The jungle disappeared and there was no shade. Pinta Island became a desert.

'Over time, I changed as well. I became an adult. During the cool nights when I was inside my shell, I became all tingly when I thought about Sentida who slept next to me. I thought about the wrinkly skin around her neck and legs, her smooth shell and her small nostrils... I fell in love.

'I started to behave like an idiot. I gazed at the moon at night, asking her to speak to Sentida for me. I wandered alone around the island composing poems, but couldn't think of a word that rhymed with tortoise.

'I was living in a fantasy world in which I had saved Pinta Island. I was a hero. Sentida and I were sitting together in a sea of yellow cotton wool.

'Then one day I woke up from my dreams.

'I saw that the island was bare. The jungle had disappeared. The goats had eaten everything. All that

George the Tortoise

was left was dry grass, cacti and bare rocks. I shouted: "No! It's not possible! Sentida? Sentida, where are you?" But Sentida was not there. Lost again? Everyone had left. Everyone.

'Only I had survived, deep in my shell, with my poems of moonlight and dreams.

'Around me lay empty shells. All the turtles had died.

'I searched for long time for the empty shell of my Sentida.

'Finally, I sat down on the rocks and gazed at the sea. I wished that tortoises could cry. I recited my second rate poems that Sentida would never hear. But then I heard a quiet voice.

"George? George, is that you?"

'I turned around. It was her. It was really her. She poked her head and her legs out of the shell next to all the empty shells. She came over to me and whispered: "I am so weak. I thought I was dead."

'I whispered: "But you are not dead." And then I believe we kissed each other.

'At that time, just offshore a boat arrived and stopped nearby. Humans came to our island. Sentida hid inside her shell. But I could not hide anymore. I walked over to the humans. I wanted to tell them my opinion about the stupid idea with the goats. But these were not the humans who had brought the goats, they were different.

They simply carried me off to their boat and I was too weak to resist. I shouted: "Sentida!" I don't know if she could hear me. The boat left. We sailed into the endless blue and I didn't know what to do.

'The last female tortoise of my kind sat on Pinta Island and would now starve to death.'

'Did she starve to death?' asked Thomas. George looked at him for a long time.

'What do you believe?' he asked finally. Thomas slowly shook his head. 'I don't think so. You have such a mysterious grin on your face.'

'You haven't asked for the treasure. The ten thousand dollar treasure.'

Thomas nodded. 'I had forgotten about it.'

'You are making progress', said George.

'In what?'

'In forgetting the unimportant things. Dollars are unimportant. You can't buy a female giant tortoise for ten thousand dollars. But this is exactly what humans try to do. Ask Camilla. And come again tomorrow, I will be waiting for you.'

Just like before, Camilla sat at the entrance. Today she chewed on her hair. 'Did you get the answer?' she asked him.

'I believe he needs a female of his own kind.'

'There isn't one. We offered ten thousand dollars to

anyone who could bring one to us. Nobody did. On Isabella Island someone found a tortoise that perhaps is related to an Abingdonii. The whole island was searched. But no, nothing. There is no female of this species left alive.'

'Perhaps there is,' said Thomas. 'And I believe I know someone who knows where she is.'

'What?'

'Give me a little more time,' he asked her. 'George is a stubborn old gentleman. It is not easy to extract things from him. But he sends his regards.' He swallowed. 'Would you go for dinner with me tonight?'

She nodded. 'Did George suggest you ask me?'

'Indirectly,' said Thomas.

* * *

The sun at the equator was shining as hot as usual on the third day of Dr Thomas Harlow's visit. But suddenly he felt that he was in the right place. The sea was infinite and blue.

'George,' he said when he climbed into the tortoise compound. 'I am thinking silly things.'

'You are in love,' said George. He seemed to be grinning.

'Tell me about the treasure', begged Thomas. 'Tell me

about Sentida. She is the treasure, isn't she?'

'Of course,' answered George. 'They brought me here to Santa Cruz. They looked after me. They gave me food to eat. And many researchers came to study me. I became famous but I was not happy. Every night I dreamt about Sentida, alone on Pinta Island. At full moon I sat in my enclosure and asked the big white tortoise of the moon to look after her.

'On one of these full moon nights, I believed I heard her voice. "George!" she called very quietly. "George! I am here!"

"Are you a dream?" I asked

"Turn your head!" said the voice in the dream. "To the right. No left! I still don't know right from left."

'I turned my head and saw her in the shadow of the research centre. I found a hole in fence and escaped through it. We both left the centre together.

'Sentida spoke. "I was with you on the boat. I smuggled myself on board when nobody was watching. I was hiding underneath a pile of ropes. I arrived with you at Santa Cruz. But unfortunately, I walked off in the wrong direction!" We laughed together as we did when we were small tortoises. And it's possible that we kissed again. We talked all night long. When it was morning, some men approached calling my name. Sentida was so terrified that she walked off.

George the Tortoise

'They put me back into my enclosure and fixed the hole in the fence. And from then on there was no chance to escape. The humans said: "We were so worried about you. What if something had happened to you? What if you had lost your way? What if you hadn't found any food?"

"I don't lose my way. I am not Sentida." But they didn't hear that.

'From that day on, Sentida visited me at every full moon. And we kissed through the fence even though it was a bit difficult.

"Let them catch you!" I whispered. "They only want us to multiply. You could join me and once you've laid some eggs, they will let us go. You will see!"

'She shook her head. The wrinkles around her neck were so beautiful. "I am frightened of humans," she whispered.

"I'm staying here where I am free. You must come out to me. You must find a way."

'But I didn't find a way. And every full moon night I begged her to let herself be caught. And every time, she said no. But still she came. I think those were our best years.

'Those years turned into decades, and we became old.

'Slowly, things changed. "George, I love you," turned into "George, eat more lettuce." "George, please escape," became, "George be careful you have a weak heart. George do this and George do that. George, don't bathe in the dirty pool. George, move into your shell or you will catch a cold. George, don't go into the sun so much."

'I did not enjoy the full moon anymore. She even spoke to other female tortoises about me. She told them they should keep an eye on me because I was not young anymore.'

'But where is she?' asked Thomas finally. 'You said Sentida is the treasure, didn't you? And you said you knew where she is. Where?'

'Well,' said George and looked into the distance.

'Well, what?'

'I've changed my mind.' said George. 'I'm not going to tell you. I would like to have a bit more peace. Only a little while; a couple of days: maybe a few years. We can get very old us tortoises, we can live to 200 years old, I believe. There is no hurry. I would like to enjoy the peace and quiet. Eating unhealthy things. Bathing in dirty water. When the time is right, I will tell Camilla where Sentida is.'

Thomas leaned over George very close to his old head. 'Tell me where she is!' he whispered insistently. 'Tell me now! You have enjoyed your peace for long enough!'

George closed his mouth and looked at Thomas, stubbornly holding his tongue.

Camilla walked up behind him and asked: 'Have you found out anything? Do you know where she is?'

George the Tortoise

Then George put his head to the side and winked at him.

'Camilla,' said Thomas and climbed out of the enclosure. 'I have to tell you something.'

'What?'

He took a deep breath. 'There are two things. First, I—I love you.'

'Oh,' said Camilla. 'Will you be staying here then?'

'Perhaps. I am going to think about that. It depends if you are going to force me to eat lettuce when we grow old.'

She laughed. 'Perhaps. I will think about it. And second?'

'Do you promise that you won't get angry with me?'

'I promise.'

He took her hands in his and looked briefly at George who looked terrific for an elderly gentleman tortoise. He winked at him.

'Second—I can't really talk to animals.'

Tiger, Tiger

by Lauren St John

Most days Caleb was still a football field's length from Shadow Alley when he had to pause, take a shuddering breath and shove his hands deep into his pockets. It was the only way he could keep them from shaking. Today, though, he'd promised himself it would be different. *He'd* be different. His birthday would change things.

'You're eleven now, Caleb, and you need to grow up and stop being a crybaby,' he told himself. 'Pa's gone and you're the man of the house.'

It was late afternoon but the sun baked down on his thin brown shoulders. The sky and the landscape were the colour of old clothes. The rain fell less often with each passing year. Eventually it would stop altogether and then the world really would end, just as they'd claimed it would all those years ago when the oil ran out.

Passing the scarred outline of concrete and mangled metal that had once been the zoo, Caleb tried to bolster his courage by imagining the strength of will it must have taken for lions, bears and tigers to spend a lifetime imprisoned in tiny cages, like murderers or thieves, far from the jungles or African wilderness of their birth. Caleb had never seen such a wild animal except in books. Outside of a few reserves and zoos, most were extinct. Caleb couldn't understand what sort of people his parents' generation and that of his grandparents and great-parents must have been to stand by and allow creatures as heart-stoppingly beautiful as a snow leopard, a jaguar, a golden eagle, a dolphin, or an oryx gazelle to be wiped from the face of the earth by hunters and quack medicine men, but they had.

'We thought they'd always be there,' his mother would say with a shrug when he asked her about it. 'We kept waiting for someone to save them.'

'Why didn't *you* save them?' Caleb wanted to know.

'I wish I had,' she'd told him sadly. 'I wish I had.'

The animal Caleb would have most like to have seen was a tiger, but the tigers had escaped and most of the other zoo inmates either starved to death or had been lost to illness or fighting during the last Water War, back when Caleb was three. His father had been killed in battle not long afterwards, defending the local lake. Now the lake was all dried up. To Caleb, it was as if he'd died for nothing.

The tigers had died for nothing too. They'd fled into the mountains, where they'd been cornered by Levi and his dad. Levi couldn't have been more than ten at the time, but he claimed to have shot a pouncing tiger as his dad finished off the other one. The skins were said to be magnificently displayed in their mansion.

At the thought of Levi, Caleb swallowed hard and shoved his hands deep into his pockets. It didn't work.

The closer he got to Shadow Alley, the more he trembled. He was tempted to run home with some excuse about how the flour seller at the market was ill, but his mother, who knew nothing of the horrors of the underpass, would only send him back the following day and he'd have to run the gauntlet again.

In Shadow Alley, it was cool, airless and dark. Caleb smelled Levi's cologne before he saw him. Every hair on his body stood on end. He put his head down and walked quickly and purposefully towards the silvery shaft of daylight at the far end.

'I'm eleven now,' he reminded himself. 'Nobody can touch me, nobody can touch me, nobody can touch me.'

'Why the hurry, Caleb?' asked Jeb, stepping out in front of him. At seventeen, the Sandler boy was all muscle and no sense. It was like being confronted by a boulder.

'Yeah, Caleb, why the rush?' demanded Zach, Jeb's smarter, slimmer twin.

'Leave me alone,' Caleb pleaded.

Levi strolled from the shadows. He was a year older than the brothers and as handsome as a Greek god. It was only on closer inspection that you could see that his eyes were flat and hard and his mouth sulky and spoiled.

'I wish we could,' he told Caleb, 'but, you see, Jeb here is bored and that can be dangerous. Zach and I like to keep him entertained and we think you can help us. Plus, it'll be lots of fun for you. So how about it? Why don't we play: Where shall we go today?'

'No!' To Caleb's shame, his eyes filled with tears. He was sweating with terror. 'I don't want to play. Please let me go. I only want to buy flour at the market.'

Levi grinned. Nothing gave him more pleasure than watching people squirm or beg. 'Of course you can go to the market, Caleb,' he said. 'But not today. Today we're going on a little journey. A magical mystery tour. We think you need a little fun in your life, Caleb. We think you need to grow up and be a man.'

* * *

Forty days and forty nights. That's what they told him as they drove away and left him to his fate, and the only thing Caleb was proud of was that he'd somehow managed to keep from crying until the sound of their engine faded and he was alone in the vast, blue-grey emptiness of the mountains. Then he didn't just cry, he sobbed, because in the end they'd taken everything from him—and this time they might just have cost him his life.

They'd started by stealing his school fees and books from him on the very first day of term. His mother, who with Caleb's assistance, scraped a meager living running a bakery from their kitchen, had saved for months to raise the funds for her son to attend the local school. He hadn't had the heart to tell her that he'd been robbed of all of it. Consequently, he set off every weekday morning as if he was going to class, and spent the day hiding in an old barn, hot and hungry. To keep his mind occupied, he'd invent lessons he could tell his mother about in the evening.

It wasn't that Caleb had been singled out for bullying. Shadow Alley divided the old and new sections of the town. For the past two years, Levi and his friends had controlled the underpass like highwaymen, taking what they pleased and beating up anyone who resisted, regardless of age or status. Their favourite game was 'Where Shall We Go Today?' Twice before Caleb had fallen victim to it. Once they'd put him in the metal scoop of a builder's crane, raised it up to two hundred feet and left him there overnight. Another time, they'd blindfolded him, shoved him into a sack, and dumped him on the rubbish tip in the next town. It had taken Caleb nearly two days to get home, stinking and covered in flies. His mother had been out of her mind with worry.

'Please don't do this,' he'd begged when it became clear that they were serious about subjecting him to what Levi called a "test of manhood" by leaving him in one of the bleakest, most inhospitable mountain ranges in the country with nothing more than a box of matches and a single bottle of water. 'My mum needs me to help her in the bakery. She's old and her health is not good. If she thinks I am missing or dead, the shock could kill her.'

'Well now, we wouldn't want your mother on our conscience,' scoffed Levi as he bit into a lamb chop. When Levi's electric-powered Land Rover had climbed as high as it could go on the crumbling mountain road, he'd parked on a flattish section of gravel and Jeb and Zach had cooked up a meaty feast on a makeshift barbecue. Caleb had never eaten anything that came from an animal, but the cooking smells were a torturous reminder of how hungry he was. His captors ate without offering him any food, however, leaving him tied up and shivering as the sun set and a mountain chill descended.

Blood dribbled down Levi's chin and he licked it up greedily. 'Don't worry, Caleb,' he said, 'I'll tell your mum that you're going to be working for my father for the next forty days. She won't even miss you.'

It took Caleb all the courage he possessed to say: 'She'll want to know where my wages are. When I come home, I mean.'

Levi gave an impatient growl and drop-kicked the lambchop bone off the edge of the mountain. 'You're not going to be going home, you idiot,' he muttered under his breath.

Zach said: 'Maybe forty days is too long, Levi. He's a runt of a kid. He could starve or be eaten by one of the feral creatures out here.'

Jeb threw his head back and laughed like a deranged hyena.

Levi rolled his eyes. 'And your point is?'

'How much are you going to pay me?' Caleb asked again. He wanted to keep them talking in the hope that they'd change their minds about abandoning him to almost certain death.

Zach grinned. 'Yeah, Levi, if he survives the forty days without his mommy, how much are you going to pay him?'

Levi mentioned a sum so large that Caleb gasped. It was more than his mother's bakery earned in a whole year.

Levi jingled his car keys as Jeb stamped out the fire. 'There's a condition,' he told Caleb with an evil smile. 'You have to be alive to collect the money. If you're dead, it doesn't count.' He climbed into the Land Rover, still laughing.

An hour after they'd driven away and left him in the eerie dark of the mountains, freed from his bonds but with nothing but his matches and bottle of water to sustain him, the cruel jeers of the three still echoed in

Caleb's ears. He had no hope of being rescued. Apart from the occasional hunter, nobody ever came to these mountains. Few people were wealthy enough to afford an electric four-wheel drive vehicle capable of making the climb and there'd be no other reason to visit such a barren, hostile place. Unless his captors had an uncharacteristic attack of conscience, he was on his own.

Caleb sniffed, dried his eyes on his sleeve and looked up at the rocky outcrop above him. In amongst the crags and scrub were several caves. For as long as he could remember, there'd been rumours among the townspeople that feral and mutant predators—some from the old zoo—stalked the mountains. He would have liked to use a cave to shelter from the night wind, but dared not risk it. Instead he stoked up the remnants of his tormentors' fire and lay down beside it. In spite of the extreme cold and his very real fear that he could die of hypothermia or be attacked by wild beasts before morning, he was asleep and dreaming almost instantly.

In the dream, he was an observer in a post-apocalyptic, Middle Eastern landscape of unrelenting bleakness. Apart from a hot breeze sifting through the dust, nothing stirred. Out of nowhere, a boy of about thirteen appeared. He walked away down the main street, his back to Caleb. He was small for his age but very strong, and clad only in a loincloth and dusty sandals. A sleeve of arrows was slung across his shoulders.

Some invisible enemy began to throw stones at him. Without looking round, he deflected them with the palm of his hand. The stones were followed by arrows, but the boy never used his own to fight back. He simply continued his calm, purposeful walk. Even when gunfire shattered the silence, the boy never broke his stride. He deflected bullets and, later, missiles, as effortlessly as a character in a video game. They glanced off the palm of his hand. Eventually, the biggest bomb on earth was sent to destroy him. The boy dispatched it as if it were nothing.

He'd now reached the end of the street. All was still and quiet. As Caleb watched, the boy sat down on the steps of a ruined building. Over the roofs behind him came a tiger. Against the beige of the surroundings, its burnished burnt-orange and jet-black-striped coat seemed to blaze like a naked flame. Caleb tried to yell a warning. The boy had survived every weapon that the world could throw at him, but he was no match for the tiger stealing up behind him.

The tiger jumped onto the step. The boy reached out and put his arm around the beast and cuddled it, and Caleb realized with awe that the tiger was the boy's friend. It was then that Caleb had a premonition. He saw that in the future tigers would once again roam the earth and he would walk among them, unafraid.

Tiger, Tiger

* * *

So real was the dream that when Caleb woke to find a tiger looking down on him, he just smiled and murmured: 'You're as magnificent as I always imagined you'd be.'

The tiger snarled and snapped at Caleb's jugular vein in a way that caused his heart to stop beating for at least a minute before it started up again, irregularly. He had time to think, 'So Levi and his dad lied about killing the tigers—or at least one of them,' before the tiger grabbed him by the belt and began hauling him up the mountain. Bumping along the gravel in the rosy glow of dawn, Caleb felt peculiarly unafraid. The dream had left him peaceful. If the tiger was planning to eat him, there was not a lot he could do about it.

The cave had a leathery, mossy smell to it. Once inside, the tiger did not eat Caleb right away but lay down and contemplated him with a slightly puzzled air. Caleb, for his part, lay unmoving, drinking in the beauty of the animal: its strength, its grace, its huge paws, green eyes and dramatic colouring. He did not pray to be spared by it. Rather he prayed that he would live as long as possible so he could savour every second he spent in its presence.

An hour went by and nothing happened. The tiger watched him and he watched the tiger. But as the temperature rose, he became increasingly hungry and thirsty. He thought of his bottle of water. Could he get it without being attacked? He stood up. The tiger bared its fangs but did nothing more. Caleb set off down the mountain, followed at a distance by the tiger. Beside the ashes of the fire, he found his bottle of water. It had been broken in the night by marauding beasts, possibly attracted by the meat bones. Caleb knew very well that without water, he'd be dead in days.

He looked at the tiger. 'Where do you drink?' he asked her. 'Where do you find water?'

The tiger growled, but it was not a growl of rage. It returned to its cave, with Caleb following. Together they spent a long, quiet, hot day. However, Caleb was used to those. He thought about his mother and hoped that Levi had done as he promised and she wasn't worrying. In the afternoon, the tiger got up and climbed the mountain, keeping to the shadows. Caleb went after her. She entered a narrow space between two rocks and set off along a dank, claustrophobic tunnel. Suddenly the space widened and became lighter. Caleb's mouth dropped open in amazement. They had entered in a vast cavern illuminated by a shaft of sunlight. In the centre of it was a spring that fed a clear pool.

The tiger immersed herself in the water. After a moment's hesitation, Caleb did the same, drinking his fill as he did so. Thirst quenched, he and the tiger lay studying one another. Caleb would willingly have drowned in the sacred green depths of the tiger's eyes. It was beyond his comprehension that Levi and his father could have taken the life of her mate.

When darkness fell, they returned to the cave. The tiger disappeared for a long while and reappeared with a rabbit she had killed for food. When she had eaten her fill, she seemed to have no objections to Caleb taking the rest. She watched as he built a fire at the cave entrance and cooked it. The eating of meat, of flesh, was repellant to him, but he knew it was his only chance of survival.

The tiger enjoyed the warmth of the fire. The flames lent a fiery sheen to her coat. When Caleb grew tired, he lay down beside her, resting his face against the silken fur of her muscular shoulder. In his dreams he thought he could hear her purring.

For forty days and forty nights, this was the pattern of their existence. They swam, they ate, they slept, they enjoyed one another's company. Caleb marked the passage of time with small stones. When at last a plume of dust signaled the return of the Land Rover, he wept not with fear—he knew he would never be afraid again—but because the most magical month of his life was almost over. He and the tiger hid in the darkest corner of the cave. Outside, he could hear the teenagers arguing as they searched for him.

Levi said: 'I don't know why we're even bothering to look for his bones. That little runt couldn't have survived a storm in a teacup. Let's tell his mother he was abducted by water raiders and hasn't been seen since.'

The tiger growled.

'What was that?' asked Zach, alarmed. 'It sounded like a wild cat.'

Levi marched into the cave, the twins following reluctantly behind. 'Well, it won't be anything larger than somebody's missing moggie,' he assured his friend. 'My father and I have shot everything else.'

The tiger gave a savage roar. She would have clawed the three in an instant had Caleb not kept a soothing arm around her. The roar echoed around the cave, causing the teenagers to scream like girls.

'Calm down,' Caleb instructed from the shadows. An idea had come to him.

'Caleb!' cried Levi looking around frantically. 'You nearly scared the life out of us. Why are you making that hideous noise? Where are you? I can't see a thing in here.'

The tiger snarled again. 'You mean, why do I sound like a tiger?' Caleb asked. 'Simple. After you left me here to die, my body was inhabited by the spirit of the tigers you killed. You remember them, don't you, Levi? You had at least one of them stuffed and mounted, and it's hanging on a wall in your home. I hate to be the bearer of bad news, Levi, but the spirit of that tiger wants revenge.'

Jeb cried: 'Didn't I tell you that them stuffed tigers always look at me funny?'

Levi went white. 'You're lying, Caleb,' he accused. 'I don't know how you're still alive, you little weasel, but when I get my hands on you, you'll be sorry.'

Caleb lit a match. He'd positioned himself so that his head was concealed by the tiger's. When the yellow light flared, Levi and the twins saw a tiger's head on a boy's body.

There were more screams. The match went out.

'It was my dad, not me,' cried Levi. 'He shot one of the tigers and wounded the other one and I guess it probably died from its injuries. We bought an extra tiger skin on the internet. I'm sorry, tiger spirit. I'm so, so sorry. Please don't hurt me. Caleb, ask it to eat Jeb instead. He has more meat on his bones.'

'What does it have to do with Jeb?' Zach said angrily. 'He didn't shoot any tigers.'

'Yeah, I don't wanna be no dinner for no tiger,' protested Jeb.

The tiger pulled from Caleb's grasp and let out another blood curdling roar.

Levi burst into tears. 'Make it stop,' he pleaded with Caleb. 'What does it want? What do *you* want?'

'We only want what's fair,' replied Caleb. 'The tiger spirit wants to be left in peace on this mountain, with no one disturbing her ever. As for me, I want the money you promised my mother...'

'It's in the Land Rover,' interrupted Zach. 'Levi tried to get out of bringing it on the grounds that you were likely to be dead, but I told him a promise was a promise. I said that if you survived forty days in this hellhole, you'd have earned it.'

'Take the money,' Levi sobbed. 'It's all yours.'

'That's not all,' said Caleb. 'I also want my school fees and books and I want you and your two thugs to agree never to hurt or bother anyone passing through Shadow Alley ever again.'

'Fine,' sniffed Levi.

'Agreed,' said Zach.

'Uh huh,' grunted Jeb.

Under cover of darkness Caleb hugged the tiger, pressing his face to her silken fur. Tears ran down his face and it seemed to him that she was crying too. One day, tigers would roam the earth again and he'd walk among them unafraid, but until then, they were on their own.

He stepped from the shadows and the teenagers gasped. In the forty days he'd spent with the tiger, Caleb had changed from a boy to a man and filled out with muscle, but that was not what shocked them. What surprised them the most was that he had an aura of invincibility about him. Strength and calmness emanated from him.

'Let's go,' he told them in a tone that brooked no argument. 'My mum will be expecting me.'

Levi stumbled wordlessly after him, like a man who has found himself in one of his own nightmares. Zach and Jeb plied him with questions. How had he survived? What had he eaten? Why did he look so fit and well and confident? What was his secret?

Caleb said nothing. He just climbed into the Land Rover and counted his 'wages.' He couldn't wait to see his mother's face light up when he walked in the door with money that would transform their lives for the first time since his father died. He couldn't wait to go to school again. But although he was looking forward to a fresh, bright start, and a big plate of his mum's vegetarian food, nothing could erase the agony he felt at being parted from the best friend he'd ever had. His heart felt as if it were being ripped from his chest. He knew even then that he would have laid down his own life for her.

Absorbed in his own thoughts, he barely noticed the engine start up, and it was not until they were bounding down the rough road that he realized Levi wasn't with them.

'It's time he had a taste of his own medicine,' Zach was saying. 'Forty days and forty nights. Let's see if he makes it.'

Caleb sat up. 'No,' he cried. 'He'll never survive. Don't leave him out here.'

'You're kidding, aren't you?' said Zach. 'If you can do it, so can he. That was our challenge to him. Don't worry, we won't really abandon him for forty days, even if he deserves it for offering Jeb to the tiger spirit for a meal. We'll come back and get him in the morning. By then he'll have learned his lesson.'

Before they rounded the first bend, Caleb looked back. Silhouetted on the boulder behind Levi was the tiger. It could have been a trick of the light but it seemed to Caleb that, as the eighteen-year-old set off in the direction of the cave, swagger gone, the tiger was eyeing him with more than a modicum of interest.

The Bear
Who Wasn't There

by Raffaella Barker

Once upon a time, not so very long ago, and not so far away, a little bear was playing snowballs with some children when he lost his way home. The cub, whose name was Arcas, hopped and tumbled for a while, waiting for the children to come and find him. No one came. He began to shiver. Even though he was a bear cub, with the thickest warmest coat you ever saw and shining eyes as dark and sweet as treacle, he was frightened to be out alone at dusk. He was happy when he was playing close to his friends. Arcas's best friends were the children. He loved their piping voices and their laughter, he loved how the tiny ones spun and floated like dandelion flowers when they played on the swing and the wooden see-saw. He crinkled his bear eyes and smiled when the older ones wrapped loving arms around his neck and breathed warmly into his fur. The children were always there. Whenever Arcas sauntered out of the woods and across the road to Main Street, some of them would be there ready to play. Before the people came, before houses were built and warmth gleamed in the windows, and gold wrapped chocolates sparkled on the Christmas trees at snow time, he had been a lonely bear cub, living with his mother Callista in a shadowy den on the edge of the woods where the hill drops away to the river. Arcas had listened to the rushing of the stream. He heard skylarks far above and the wind in the trees of his homeland. He heard the emptiness, the echoing silence. And he was sad.

Once, many bears had lived in these dens, which interlocked like honeycomb on the edge of the tangled wood above town somewhere not so far away. The young bears tumbled and somersaulted in the pastures. They climbed trees for berries in the woods. They dived into the river to catch a silver fish and bat it with their paws, throwing it from one to another until some smart cub— on the cusp of growing up—would duck down, open wide and swallow that fish in one gulp. Arcas knew this because Callista had told him. Every winter, he and his mother snuggled into their den as the days grew grey and cold. Callista fed him nuts and honey to fill him with goodness for his long sleep, and told him stories of his ancestors. What she didn't tell him though, was what had happened next.

Arcas was cold and tired. He tried to call to the children, but his snuffles and his whispered roar went nowhere in the muffled silence of falling snow. He only ever whispered his roar because otherwise he knew it would frighten the children. They were so small with their pink cheeks and smiling faces. Three of them would climb up on his back for a ride, hugging themselves close to him, urging him to run and whoosh and slide through the fields and hills around town.

'You are our dream bear, we wished you here and you came, just like it said in our books,' they cried. 'We love you Arcas.' He loved them too, and now he had lost them, and he hadn't said goodbye before tomorrow's sleep began.

The lights of the town disappeared. Arcas was in a silver landscape, trotting towards nothing he recognised. He howled suddenly, he couldn't help himself, he was scared. How would he be found? His mother was out gathering berries, she had told him that morning she would not be home until late.

'Arcas you can go and play all day, for tomorrow we start our winter sleep. I will bring the final part of our feast and tomorrow we will dig ourselves in deep until spring.' Arcas loved waking up in spring, trees were green, the river rushed with sparkling water and the children would be waiting for him, ready to play. But where was he now? Arcas saw a dark grove of what looked like nut trees. His mother might be there. He trotted in.

He found himself in a cave, not in a grove of trees at all. He crouched and fumbled on the ground, stumbling over some stones. He remembered his mother preparing for hibernation with him, and he struck the stones together and made a spark. Then he lit a torch. He was not in a shallow cave, he was deep in a maze of chambers like his own den, but unused. Curious, though his heart thumped as loud as a hammer on a sheet of tin, he shuffled further into the cave, and through a tunnel to the next one. There, his torch lit wall paintings. He stopped and stared in horror. There were hunters with spears, dozens of them, pursuing bears as they ran to shelter. There were pictures of bears trapped in nets and being dragged away in chains. There were bears dancing in front of faceless crowds, tall on their hind legs, eyes sad, fur matted. Arcas stared at them for some time, his eyes wide and shocked. He had never understood where all the ancestor bears his mother told him about had gone, and now he could see it for himself. The final painting was of a bigger bear, up on his hind legs, roaring and swiping the air with his claws. Swirling up from his paws were stars. Above him on the ceiling of the cave the stars had formed into bears in the sky. Arcas was relieved to see these bears: they looked happy.

Soon the torch guttered and the flame was swallowed by darkness. Arcas gave a little grunt of fear and made his way back towards the entrance. His eyes adjusted to the darkness, and he stumbled, but to keep himself steady he fixed his mind on the star bears on the ceiling. Outside the cave, night had fallen. Snow glistened and the moon was up and brightly shining. Arcas's breath made a cloud when he howled again for his mother. She didn't come. He thought he heard a rustling ahead of him in the forest and he scampered in, calling 'Mother, mother where are you?' His voice echoed around him. His mother should be home by now, but which way was home? Pine trees stretched in all directions around him, every one looked familiar but wasn't. Arcas was lost.

Arcas may have been a small bear, but he was resourceful and brave. The tallest tree you ever saw stood at the centre of a clearing in front of him. It was a redwood tree, and its trunk was as wide and huge as a cathedral spire rising before him. Arcas reached his paws to the lowest branches and hoisted himself up. He began to climb. It was a joyful feeling, skimming up the redwood tree. Soon he was high above the other trees in the forest, hugging the trunk, inching his way up and up to the top. The air was cold at the top of the tree, and the night sky floated above the forest like an inky scarf scattered with diamonds. Arcas felt weightless and free. He could see the happy star bears from the cave paintings gambolling and playing on the horizon, and the star path which his mother had told him was called the Milky Way shimmered ahead of him. It was then he saw Callista, twinkling at him from the top of the world. Suddenly he knew what to do. He stretched out his tiny tail to balance himself, and he shut his eyes. Taking a deep breath, Arcas stepped out onto the Milky Way and he walked into the night sky towards his mother.

The River Nemunas

by Anthony Doerr

I'm fifteen years old. My parents are dead. I have a poodle named Mishap in a pet carrier between my ankles and a biography of Emily Dickinson in my lap. The flight attendant keeps refilling my apple juice. I'm thirty-six thousand feet over the Atlantic Ocean. Outside my little smudgy window, the whole world has turned to water.

I'm moving to Lithuania. Lithuania is in the upper right corner of Europe. Over by Russia. On the world map at school, Lithuania is pink.

Grandpa Z is waiting for me outside baggage claim. His belly looks big enough to fit a baby inside. He hugs me for a long time. Then he lifts Mishap out of his carrier and hugs Mishap, too.

Lithuania doesn't look pink. More like grey. Grandpa Z's little Peugeot is green and smells like rock dust. The sky sits low over the highway. We drive for a long time, past hundreds of half-finished concrete apartment buildings that look like they've been set here by the retreat of a huge flood. There are big Nokia signs and bigger Aquafresh signs.

Grandpa Z says, Aquafresh is good toothpaste. You have Aquafresh in Kansas?

I tell him we used Colgate.

He says, I find you Colgate.

We merge onto on a four-lane divided highway. The land on both sides is broken into pastures that look awfully muddy for early July. It starts to rain. The Peugeot has no windshield wipers. Mishap dozes in my lap. Lithuania turns a steamy green. Grandpa Z drives with his head out the window.

Eventually we stop at a house with a peaked wooden roof and a central chimney. It looks exactly like the twenty other houses crowded in around it.

Home, says Grandpa Z, and Mishap jumps out.

The house is long and narrow, like a train car. Grandpa Z has three rooms: a kitchen in front, a bedroom in the middle, and a bathroom in the back. Outside there's a shed. He unfolds a card table. He brings me a little stack of Pringles on a plate. Then a steak. No green beans, no dinner rolls, nothing like that. We sit on the edge of his bed to eat. Grandpa Z doesn't say grace so I whisper it to myself. Bless us O Lord and these, thy gifts. Mishap sniffs around skeptically between my feet.

Halfway through his steak Grandpa Z looks up at me and there are tears on his cheeks.

It's okay, I say. I've been saying it's okay a lot lately. I've said it to church ladies and flight attendants and counsellors. I say, I'm fine. It's okay. I don't know if I'm fine or if it's okay, or if saying it makes anyone feel better. Mostly it's just something to say.

Anthony Doerr

* * *

It was cancer. In case you were wondering. First they found it in Mom and she got her breasts cut off and her ovaries cut out but it was still in her, and then Dad got tested and it was in his lungs. I imagined cancer as a tree: a big, black, leafless tree inside Mom and another inside Dad. Mom's tree killed her in May. Dad's killed him three weeks later.

I'm an only child and have no other relatives so the lawyers sent me to live with Grandpa Z. The Z is for Zydrunas.

Grandpa Z's bed is in the kitchen because he's giving me the bedroom. The walls are bare plaster and the bed groans and the sheets smell like dust on a hot bulb. There's no shade on the window. On the dresser is a brand-new pink panda, which is sort of for babies, but also sort of cute. A price tag is still pinned to its ear: 39.99 L. The L is for Litas. I don't know if 39.99 is a lot or a little.

After I turn off the lamp, all I see is black. Something goes tap tap tap against the ceiling. I can hear Mishap panting at the foot of the bed. My three duffel bags, stacked against the wall, contain everything I own in the world.

Do I sound faraway? Do I sound lost? Probably I am.

The River Nemunas

I whisper: Dear God, please watch over Mom in Heaven and please watch over Dad in Heaven and please watch over me in Lithuania. And please watch over Mishap, too. And Grandpa Z.

And then I feel the Big Sadness coming on, like there's a shiny and sharp axe blade buried inside my chest. The only way I can stay alive is to remain absolutely motionless so instead of whispering Dear God how could you do this to me, I only whisper Amen which Pastor Jenks back home told me means I believe. I lay with my eyelids closed clutching Mishap and inhaling his smell, which always smells to me like corn chips and practice breathing in light and breathing out a color—light, green, light, yellow—like the counsellor told me to do when the panic comes.

* * *

At 4 am the sun is already up. I sit in a lawn chair beside Grandpa's shed and watch Mishap sniff around in Lithuania. The sky is silver and big scarves of mist drag through the fields. A hundred little black birds land on the roof of Grandpa's shed, then take off again.

Each house in Grandpa Z's little cluster of houses has lace curtains in the windows. The houses are all the same but the lace is different in each one. One has a floral pattern, one a linear pattern, and another has circles butted up against each other. As I look, an old woman pushes aside a zig-zag-patterned curtain in one of the windows. She puts on a pair of huge glasses and waves me over. I can see there are tubes hooked through her nose.

Her house is twenty feet away from Grandpa Z's and it's full of Virgin Mary statues and herbs and smells like carrot peels. In the back room, a man in a tracksuit is asleep on a bed. The old lady unhooks herself from a machine that looks like two scuba tanks hung on a wheeled rack. She pats the couch and says a bunch of words to me in Russian. Her mouth is full of gold. She has a marble-sized mole under her right eye. Her calves are like bowling pins and her toes look beaten and crushed.

She nods at something I don't say and turns on a massive flat-screen television propped up on two cinderblocks. Together we watch a pastor give mass on TV. The colours are skewed and the audio is garbled. In his church there are maybe twenty-five people in folding chairs. When I was a baby Mom talked to me in Lithuanian so I can understand some of the pastor's sermon. There's something about his daddy falling off his roof. He says this means that just because you can't see something, doesn't mean you shouldn't believe in it. I can't tell if he means Jesus or gravity.

Afterward the old lady brings me a big hot stuffed

potato covered with bacon bits. She watches me eat through her huge, steamy eyeglasses.

Thanks, I say in Lithuanian, which sounds like achoo. She stares off into oblivion.

When I get back to Grandpa Z's house he has a magazine open in his lap with space diagrams in it.

You are at Mrs Sabo's?

I was. Past tense, Grandpa.

Grandpa Z circles a finger beside his ear. Mrs. Sabo no more remember things, he says. You understand?

I nod.

I read here, Grandpa Z says, clearing his throat, that Earth has three moons. He bites his lower lip, thinking through the English. No, it used to has three moons. Earth used to has three moons. Long time ago. What do you think of this?

* * *

You want to know? What it's like? To prop up the dam? To keep your fingers plugged in its cracks? To feel like every single breath that passes is another betrayal, another step farther away from what you were and where you were and who you were, another step deeper into the darkness? Grandpa Z came to Kansas twice this spring. He sat in the rooms and smelled the smells. Now he leans forward till I can see the little red lightning bolts of veins in his eyes. You want to speak?

No thanks, Grandpa Z.

I mean talk, he says. Talk, Allie?

No. Thanks.

No? But to talk is good, no?

Grandpa Z makes gravestones. Gravestones in Lithuania aren't quite like the ones in America. They're glossy and smooth and made of granite, but most of them are etched with likenesses of the people buried underneath them. They're like black-and-white photos carved right into the stones. They're expensive and everyone spends money on them. Poor people, Grandpa Z says, spend the most. Sometimes he etches faces while other times he does the deceased's whole body, like a tall man standing in a leather jacket, life-size, very realistic, buttons on the cuffs and freckles on the cheeks. Grandpa Z shows me a Polaroid of a tombstone he made of a famous mobster. The stone is seven feet tall and has a life-size portrait of a suited man with his hands in his pockets sitting on the hood of a Mercedes. He says the family paid extra to have a halo added around the man's head.

Monday morning Grandpa Z goes to his workshop and school doesn't start for two months so I'm left alone in the house. By noon I've looked through all

The River Nemunas

of Grandpa Z's drawers and his one closet. In the shed I find two fishing rods and an old aluminum boat under a tarp and eight jars of Lithuanian pennies and thousands of mouse-chewed British magazines: *Popular Science* and *Science Now* and *British Association for the Advancement of Physics*. There are magazines on polar bears and Mayan calendars and cell biology and lots of things I don't understand. Inside are faded cosmonauts and gorillas hooked up to machines and cartoon cars driving around on Mars.

Then Mrs Sabo shows up. She shouts something in her derelict Russian and goes over to a chest of drawers and pulls open a cigarette box and inside are photographs.

Motina, she says, and points at me.

I say, I thought you couldn't remember things.

But she is sticking the photos under my nose like she has just remembered something and wants to get it out before she forgets it. Motina means Mom. All of the photos contain Mom when she was a girl. Here she is in a polar bear costume and here she is frowning over what might be an upturned lawnmower and here she is tramping barefoot through mud.

Mrs Sabo and I lay out the pictures in a grid on Grandpa Z's card table. There are sixty-eight of them. Five-year-old Mom scowls in front of a rusted-out Soviet tank. Six-year-old Mom peels an orange. Nine-year-old

Mom stands in the weeds. Looking at the photos starts a feeling in my gut like maybe I want to dig a shallow hole in the yard and lie down in it.

I separate out twelve of the pictures. In each of them, my mom—my Subaru-driving, cashew-eating, Barry-Manilow-listening, Lithuanian-immigrant, dead-because-of-cancer Mom—is either standing in murky water or leaning over the side of a junky-looking boat, helping to hold up some part of a creepy and gigantic shark.

Erketas, Mrs Sabo says, and nods gravely. Then she coughs for about two minutes straight.

Erketas?

But by now the coughing has shaken all the comprehension of out her. The man in the tracksuit comes over and says something and Mrs Sabo stares at the lower part of his face for a while and eventually the man coaxes her back to her house. Grandpa Z comes home from his job at 2:31.

Grandpa, I say, your toilet paper might as well be made out of gravel.

He nods thoughtfully.

And is this my mom, I ask, with all these great whites?

Grandpa looks at the pictures and blinks and puts a knuckle between his teeth. For maybe thirty seconds he doesn't answer. He looks like he's standing outside an

The River Nemunas

elevator waiting for the doors to open.

Finally he says, Erketas. He goes to a book in a box on the floor and opens it and pages through it and looks up and looks back down and says, Sturgeon.

Sturgeon. Erketas means sturgeon?

River fish. From the river.

We eat sausage for dinner. No bread, no salad. All through the meal the photos of Mom stare up at us.

I rinse the dishes. Grandpa Z says, You walk with me, Allie?

He leads me and Mishap across the field behind the colony of houses. There are neat little vegetable gardens and goats staked here and there. Grasshoppers skitter out in front of us. We clamber over a fence and pick our way around cow dung and nettles. The little trail heads toward some willows and on the other side of the willows is a river: quiet and brown, surprisingly far across. At first the river looks motionless, like a lake, but the more I look, the more I see it's moving very slowly.

Mishap sneezes. I don't think he's ever seen a river before. A line of cows saunters along on the far bank.

Grandpa Z says, Fishing. Is where your mother goes. Used to go. Past tense. He laughs an unsmiling laugh. Sometimes with her grandpa. Sometimes with Mrs. Sabo.

What's it called?

The River Nemunas. It is called the River Nemunas.

* * *

Every hour the thought floats to the surface: If we're all going to end up happy together in Heaven then why does anyone wait? Every hour the Big Sadness hangs behind my ribs, sharp and gleaming, and it's all I can do to keep breathing.

Mrs Sabo, Grandpa Z says, is either 90 years old or 94 years old. Not even her son knows for sure. She has lived through the first Lithuanian independence and the second one, too. She fought with the Russians the first time, against them the second time. Back when all these houses were a communal farm under the Soviets, she used to take a rowboat every day for thirty-five years and row six miles up the river to work in a chemical plant. She went fishing when no women went fishing, he says.

Nowadays Mrs Sabo has to be hooked up to her oxygen machine every night. She doesn't seem to mind if I come over to watch TV. We turn the volume up really high to hear over the wheezing and banging of her pump. Sometimes we watch the Lithuanian pastor. Sometimes we watch cartoons. Sometimes it's so late we only watch a channel that shows a satellite map of the world, rotating forever across the screen.

* * *

The River Nemunas

I've been in Lithuania two weeks when Counsellor Mike calls on Grandpa Z's cell phone. Counsellor Mike, a lawyer who chews bubblegum and wears basketball shorts. It's two in the morning in Kansas. He asks how I'm adjusting. Hearing his wide-open American voice calls up for me, in a sudden rush, summertime Kansas. It's like it's right there on the other end of the phone, the air silky, the last porchlights switched off, a fog of gnats hovering above Brown's pond, the moon coming to earth through sheets and layers and curtains of moisture, streetlights sending soft columns of light onto grocery story parking lots. And somewhere in that sleepy darkness Counsellor Mike sits at his clunky kitchen table in his socks and asks an orphan in Lithuania how she's adjusting.

It takes me a full ten seconds to say, I'm fine, it's okay.

He says he needs to talk to Grandpa. We got an offer on the house, he says. Grown-up stuff.

Is the offer good?

Any offer is good.

I don't know what to say to that. I can hear music coming from his end, faraway and full of static. What does Counsellor Mike listen to, deep in the Kansas night?

We're praying for you, Allie, he says.

Who's we?

Us at the office. And at church. Everyone. Everyone is

praying for you.

Grandpa's at work, I say.

Then I walk Mishap across the field and over the fence and through the rocks to the river. The cows are still on the far side, eating whatever cows eat and whipping their tails back and forth.

Five thousand miles away Counsellor Mike is staying up late to plan the sale of the orange plastic tiles Dad glued to the basement floor and the dent I put in the dining room wall and the raspberry bushes Mom planted in the backyard. He's going to sell our warped baking sheets and half-used shampoos and the six Jedi drinking glasses we got from Pizza Hut that Dad said we could keep only after asking our pastor if *Star Wars* would have been 'endorsed by Jesus.' Everything, all of it, our junk, our detritus, our memories. And I've got the family poodle and three duffel bags of too-small clothes and four photo albums, but no one left who can flesh out any of the photos. I'm five thousand miles and four weeks away and every minute that ratchets past is another minute that the world has kept on turning without Mom and Dad in it. And I'm supposed to live with Grandpa Z in Lithuania, what, for the rest of my life?

Thinking about the house sitting there empty back in Kansas starts the Big Sadness swinging in my chest like a pendulum and soon a blue nothingness is creeping

The River Nemunas

around the edges of my vision. It comes on fast this time and the axe blade is slicing up organs willy-nilly and all of the sudden it feels like I'm looking into a very blue bag and someone's yanking the drawstring closed. I fall over into the willows.

I lie there for who knows how long. Up in the sky I see Dad emptying his pockets after work, dumping coins and breath mints and business cards onto the kitchen counter. I see Mom cutting a fried chicken breast into tiny white triangles and dunking each piece in ketchup. I see the Virgin Mary walk out onto a little balcony between the clouds and look around and take hold of French doors, one on either side of her, and slam them shut.

I can hear Mishap sniffing around nearby. I can hear the river sliding past and grasshoppers chewing the leaves and the sad, dreamy clanking of faraway cowbells. The sun is tiny and flame-blue. When I finally sit up, Mrs Sabo is standing beside me. I didn't know she could walk so far. Little white butterflies are looping through the willows. The river glides past. She says something in machine-gun Russian and I sit up and she sets her frozen hand on my forehead. Then we watch the river, Mrs Sabo and Mishap and me, in the grass in the sun. And as we watch the water, and breathe, and I come back into myself—I swear—a fish as big as a nuclear missile leaps out of the river. Its belly is spotless white and its back is grey. It curls up in mid-air and flaps its tail and stretches like it's thinking. This time gravity will let me go.

When it comes back down, water explodes far enough across the river that some drops land on my feet.

Mishap raises his ears, cocks his head. The river heals itself over. Mrs. Sabo looks at me from behind her huge eyeglasses and blinks her milky eyes a dozen times.

Did you see that? Please tell me you saw that.

Mrs Sabo only blinks.

Grandpa Z gets home at 3:29.

I bought you a surprise, he says. He opens the hatchback of the Peugeot and inside is a crate of American toilet paper.

Grandpa, I say. I want to go fishing.

* * *

Dad used to say God made the world and everything in it and Grandpa Z would say if God made the world and everything in it, then why isn't everything perfect? Why do we get hernias and why do beautiful healthy daughters get cancer? Then Dad would say well, God was a mystery and Grandpa Z would say God was a, what's the word, a security blanket for babies, and Dad would stomp off and Mom would throw down her

The River Nemunas

napkin and blast some Lithuanian words at Grandpa and go jogging after Dad and I'd look at the plates on the table.

Grandpa Z crossed the ocean twice this spring to watch his daughter and son-in-law die. Did God have explanations for that? Now I stand in Grandpa Z's kitchen and listen to him say that there aren't any sturgeon anymore in the River Nemunas. There might be some left in the Baltic Sea, he says, but there aren't any in the river. He says his dad used to take Mom sturgeon fishing every Sunday for years and Mrs Sabo probably caught a few in the old days but then there was overfishing and pesticides and the Kaunas dam and black-market caviar and his dad died and the last sturgeon died and the Soviet Union broke up and Mom grew up and went to university in the United States and married a creationist and no one has caught a sturgeon in the Nemunas River for twenty-five years.

Grandpa, I say, Mrs Sabo and I saw a sturgeon. Today. Right over there. And I point out the window across the field to the line of willows.

It is photos, he says. You see the photos of your mother.

I saw a sturgeon, I say. Not in a picture. In the river.

Grandpa Z closes his eyelids and opens them. Then he holds me by the shoulders and looks me in the eyes and says, We see things. Sometimes they there.

Sometimes they not there. We see them the same either way. You understand?

* * *

I saw a sturgeon. So did Mrs. Sabo. I go to bed mad and wake up mad. I throw the stuffed panda against the wall and stomp around on the porch and kick gravel in the driveway. Mishap barks at me.

In the morning I watch Grandpa Z drive off to work, big and potbellied and confused, and I can hear Mrs Sabo's machine whirring and thunking in her house next door and I think: I should have told Grandpa Z to trust me. I should have told him about the pastor's old daddy and the stepladder and Jesus and gravity and how just because you don't see something doesn't mean you shouldn't believe in it.

Instead I wade into Grandpa Z's shed and start pulling out boxes and granite samples and chisels and rock saws and it takes me a half hour to clear a path and another half hour to drag the old aluminum boat into the driveway. It's flat-bottomed and has three bench seats and there are maybe a thousand spiders living beneath each one. I blast them out with a hose. I find a bottle of some toxic Lithuanian cleaner and I pour it all over the hull.

The River Nemunas

After a while Mrs Sabo comes tottering out in her big eyeglasses and her little arms and looks at me like a praying mantis. She lets off a chain of coughs. Her son comes out in his tracksuit with a cigarette between his lips and he watches me work for ten minutes or so. Then he leads his mother back inside.

Grandpa Z gets home at 3:27. There are boxes and hoses and rakes and tools all over the driveway. The bottle of solvent has left bright, silver streaks across the hull of the boat. I say, Mrs Sabo and I saw a sturgeon in the river yesterday, Grandpa.

Grandpa Z blinks at me. He looks like maybe he's looking into the past at something he thought had ended a long time ago.

He says, No more sturgeon in the Nemunas.

I say, I want to try to catch one.

They not here, Grandpa Z says. They endangered species. It means—

I know what it means.

He looks from me to the boat to Mishap to me. He takes off his hat and drags his hand through his hair and puts his hat back on. Then he nudges the boat with the toe of his sneaker and shakes his head and Mishap wags his tail and a cloud blows out of the way. Sunlight explodes off of everything.

Anthony Doerr

* * *

I use an ancient, flat-tired dolly to drag the boat through the field and over the fence to the river. It takes me three hours. Then I lug the oars and the fishing poles down. Then I walk back and tell Mrs Sabo's son I'm taking her out on the river and guide Mrs Sabo by the arm and lead her across the field and sit her in the bow of the boat. In the sunlight her skin looks like old candle wax.

We fish with blunt, seven-foot rods and ancient hooks that are as big as my hand. We use worms. Mrs Sabo's face stays completely expressionless. The current is very slow and it's easy to paddle once in a while and keep the boat in the center of the river.

Mishap sits on the bench beside Mrs Sabo and shivers with excitement. The river slips along. We see a whole herd of feral cats sleeping on a boulder in the sun. We see a deer twitching its ears in the shallows. Black and gray and green walls of trees slide past.

In the late afternoon I pull onto what turns out to be an island and Mrs Sabo steps out of the boat and lifts up her housedress and has a long pee in the willows. I open a can of Pringles and we share it.

Did you know my mother? I ask Mrs Sabo but she only glances over at me and gives me a dreamy look. As if she knows everything but I wouldn't understand.

Her eyes are a thousand miles away. I like to think she's remembering other trips down the river, other afternoons in the sun. I read to her from one of Grandpa Z's nature magazines. I tell her a bald eagle's feathers weigh twice as much as its bones. I tell her aardvarks drink their water by eating cucumbers. I tell her that male emperor moths can smell female emperor moths flapping along six miles away.

It takes me a couple of hours of rowing to get back home. We watch big pivot sprinklers spray rainbows over a field of potatoes and we watch a thousand boxcars go rattling along behind a train. It's beautiful out here, I say.

Mrs. Sabo looks up. Remember? she asks in Lithuanian. But she doesn't say anything else.

We don't catch any fish. Mishap falls asleep. Mrs Sabo's knees get sunburned.

* * *

That one day is all it takes. Every morning Grandpa Z leaves to go carve dead people's faces into granite, and as soon as he's gone I take Mrs Sabo out in the boat. An old-timer six houses down tells me I should be using rotten hamburger meat, not worms, and that I should stuff it inside the toes of pantyhose and tie the pantyhose to the hooks with elastic thread. So I get some hamburger and put it in a bucket in the sun until it smells like hell, but the pantyhose won't stay on the hook, and a lady at the convenience store in Mažeikiai says she hasn't seen a sturgeon in fifty years but when there were sturgeon they didn't want rotten food, they wanted fresh sand shrimp on big hooks.

I try deep holes behind rapids and eddies beside fields of bright yellow flowers and big, blue, shadowy troughs. I try clams and night crawlers and—once—frozen chicken thighs. I keep thinking Mrs Sabo will pipe up, will remember, will tell me how it's done. But mostly she sits there with that long-gone look on her face. My brain gradually becomes like a map of the river bottom: gravel bars, two sunken cars with their rust-chewed rooftops just below the surface, long stretches of still water seething with trash. You'd think the surface of a river would be steady but it isn't. There are all these churnings and swirls and eddies, bubblings and blossomings, submerged stumps and plastic bags and spinning crowns of light down there, and when the sun is right sometimes you can see forty feet down.

We don't catch a sturgeon. We don't even see any. I begin to think maybe Grandpa Z is right, maybe sometimes the things we think we see aren't really what we see. But here's the surprising thing: It doesn't bother me. I like being out there with Mrs Sabo. She seems okay

The River Nemunas

with it, her son seems okay with it, and maybe I'm okay with it, too. Maybe it feels as if the wretchedness in my gut might be getting a little smaller.

When I was five I got an infection and Dr Nasser put some drops in my eyes. Pretty soon all I could see were blurs and colors. Dad was a fog and Mom was a smudge and the world looked like it does when your eyes are completely full of tears.

Four hours later, right around when Dr Nasser said it would, my eyesight came back. I was riding in the backseat of Mom's Subaru and the world started coming back into focus. I was myself again and the trees were trees again, only the trees looked more alive than I'd ever seen them: the branches above our street were interlaced beneath an ocean of leaves, thousands and thousands of leaves scrolling past, dark on the tops and pale on the undersides, every individual leaf moving independently but still in concert with the others.

Going out on the Nemunas is sort of like that. You come down the path and step through the willows and it's like seeing the lights in the world come back on.

* * *

Even when there's not much of a person left, you can still learn things about her. I learn that Mrs Sabo likes the smell of cinnamon. I learn she perks up any time we round this one particular bend in the river. Even with her little gold-capped teeth she chews food slowly and delicately, and I think maybe her mom must have been strict about that, like, Sit up straight, Chew carefully, Watch your manners. Emily Dickinson's mom was like that. Of course Emily Dickinson wound up terrified of death and wore only white clothes and would only talk to visitors through the closed door of her room.

Mid-August arrives and the nights are hot and damp. Grandpa Z keeps the windows open. I can hear Mrs Sabo's oxygen machine wheezing and murmuring all night. In half-dreams, it's a sound like the churning of the world through the universe.

Yellow, green, red runs the flag flapping in front of the post office. Sun up top, Grandpa Z says, land in the middle, blood down below. Lithuania: doormat of a thousand wars.

I miss Kansas. I miss the redbud trees, the rainstorms, how the college kids all wear purple on football Saturdays. I miss Mom walking into the grocery store and pushing her sunglasses up on her forehead, or Dad pedaling up a hill on his bicycle, me a little person in a bike trailer behind him, his maroon backpack bobbing up and down.

One day late in August Mrs Sabo and I are drifting

The River Nemunas

downstream, our lines trailing in the river, when Mrs Sabo starts talking in Lithuanian. I've known her forty days and not heard her say so much in all of them combined. She tells me that the afterworld is a garden. She says it's on a big mountain on the other side of an ocean. This garden is always warm and there are no winters there and that's where the birds go in the fall. She waits a few minutes and then says that death is a woman named Giltine. Giltine is tall, skinny, blind, and always really, really hungry. Mrs Sabo says when Giltine walks past, mirrors splinter, beekeepers find coffin-shaped honeycombs in the hives, and people dream of teeth being pulled. Anytime you have a dream about the dentist, she says, that means death walked past you in the night.

One of Grandpa Z's magazines says that when a young albatross first takes wing, it can stay in the air without touching the ground for fifteen years. I think when I die I'd like to be tied to ten thousand balloons, so I could go floating into the clouds, and get blown off somewhere above the cities, and then the mountains, and then the ocean, just miles and miles of blue ocean, my corpse sailing above it all.

Maybe I could last fifteen years up there. Maybe an albatross could land on me and use me for a little resting perch. Maybe that's silly. But it makes as much sense,

I think, as watching your Mom and Dad get buried in boxes in the mud.

* * *

At nights Mrs Sabo and I start watching a show called *Boy Meets Grill* on Mrs Sabo's big TV. I try cooking zucchini crisps and Pepsi-basted eggplant. I try cooking asparagus Francis and broccoli Diane. Grandpa Z screws up his eyebrows sometimes when he comes in the door but he sits through my Bless Us O Lord and he eats everything I cook and washes it all down with Juozo beer. And some weekends he drives me up the road to little towns with names like Panemunė and Pagėgiai and we buy ice cream sandwiches from Lukoil stations, and Mishap sleeps in the hatchback and at dusk the sky goes from blue to purple and purple to black.

Almost every day in August Mrs Sabo and I fish for sturgeon. I row upriver and drift us home, dropping our cinderblock anchor now and then to fish the deep holes. I sit in the bow and Mrs Sabo sits in the stern and Mishap sleeps under the middle bench, and I wonder about how memories can be here one minute and then gone the next. I wonder about how the sky can be a huge, blue nothingness and at the same time it can also feel like a shelter.

The River Nemunas

* * *

It's the last dawn in August. We are fishing a mile upstream from the house when Mrs Sabo sits up and says something in Russian. The boat starts rocking back and forth. Then her reel starts screaming.

Mishap starts barking. Mrs Sabo jams her heels against the hull and jabs the butt of her rod into her belly and holds on. The reel yowls.

Whatever is on the other end takes a lot of line. Mrs Sabo clings to it and doesn't let go and a strange, fierce determination flows into her face. Her glasses slide down her nose. A splotch of sweat shaped like Australia blooms on the back of her blouse. She mutters to herself in Russian. Her little baggy arms quiver. Her rod is bent into an upside-down U.

What do I do? There's nobody there to answer so I say, Pray, and I pray. Mrs Sabo's line disappears at a diagonal into the river and I can see it bending away through the water, dissolving into a coffee-colored darkness. The boat seems like it might actually be moving upriver and Mrs Sabo's reel squeaks and it feels like what the Sunday school teacher used to tell us during choir practice when she'd say we were tapping into something larger than ourselves.

Slowly the line makes a full circuit of the boat. Mrs

Sabo pulls up on her rod, and cranks her reel, gaining ground inch by inch, little by little. Then she gets a bit of slack so she starts reeling like mad, taking in yards of line, and whatever it is on the other end tries to make a run.

Bubbles rise to the surface. The swivel and weight on Mrs Sabo's line become visible. It holds there a minute, just below the surface of the water, as if we are about to see whatever is just below the leader, whatever is struggling there just beneath the surface, when, with a sound like a firecracker, Mrs Sabo's line pops and the swivel and the broken leader fly up over our heads.

Mrs Sabo staggers backward and nearly falls out of the boat. She drops the rod. Her glasses fall off. She says something like, Holy, holy, holy, holy.

Little ripples spread across the face of the river and are pulled downstream. Then there's nothing. The current laps quietly against the hull. We resume our quiet slide downriver. Mishap licks Mrs Sabo's hands. And Mrs Sabo gives me a little gold-toothed smile as if whatever was on the other end of her fishing line has just pulled her back into the present for a minute and in the silence I feel she's here, together with me, under the Lithuanian sunrise, both of us with decades left to live.

* * *

The River Nemunas

Grandpa Z doesn't believe me. He sits on the edge of his bed, elbows on the card table, a mildly-renowned Lithuanian tombstone maker, with droopy eyes and broken blood vessels in his cheeks, a plate of half-eaten cauliflower parmesan in front of him, and wipes his eyes and tells me I need to start thinking about school clothes. He says maybe we caught a carp or an old tire but that for us to catch a sturgeon would be pretty much like catching a dinosaur, about as likely as dredging a big seventy-million-year-old Triceratops up out of the river muck.

Mrs Sabo hooked one, I say.

Okay, Grandpa Z says. But he doesn't even look at me.

* * *

Mažeikiai Senamiesčcio Secondary School is made of sand-colored bricks. The windows are all black. A boy in the parking lot throws a tennis ball onto the roof and waits for the ball to roll down and catches it and does this over and over.

It looks like every other school, I say.

It looks nice, Grandpa Z says.

It starts to rain. He says, You are nervous, and I say, How come you don't believe me about the fish? He looks at me and looks back at the parking lot and rolls down the window and swipes raindrops from the windshield with his palm.

There are sturgeon in the river. Or there's one. There's at least one.

They all gone, Allie, he says. You only break your heart more with this fishing. You only make yourself more lonely, more sad.

So what, Grandpa, you don't believe in anything you can't see? You believe we don't have souls? You put a cross on every headstone that you make, but you think the only thing that happens to us when we die is that we turn into mud?

For a while we watch the kid throw and catch his tennis ball. He never misses. Grandpa Z says, I come to Kansas. I ride airplane. I see tops of all clouds. No people up there. No gates, no Jesus. Your mother and father are in the sky sitting on the clouds? You think this?

I look back at Mishap, who's curled up in the hatchback against the rain. Maybe, I say. Maybe I think something like that.

* * *

I make friends with a girl named Laima and another girl named Asta. They watch *Boy Meets Grill*, too. Their parents are not dead. Their mothers yell at them for shaving their legs and tell them things like, I really wish you wouldn't chew your hangnails like that, Laima, or, Your skirt is way too short, Asta.

At night I lie in bed with Grandpa Z's unpainted plaster slowly cracking all around me and no shade on the window and Mrs Sabo's machine wheezing next door and stars creeping imperceptibly across the windowpane and reread the part in my Emily Dickinson biography when she says, "To live is so startling it leaves little time for anything else." People still remember Emily Dickinson said that but when I try to remember a sentence Mom or Dad said, I can't remember a single one. They probably said a million sentences to me before they died but tonight it seems all I have are prayers and cliches. When I shut my eyes I can see Mom and Dad at church, Mom holding a little maroon church songbook, Dad's little yachting belt and penny loafers. He leans over to whisper something to me—a little girl standing in the pew beside him. But when his mouth opens, no sound comes out.

* * *

The willows along the river turn yellow. Our history teacher takes us on a field trip to the KGB museum in Vilnius. The KGB used to cram five or six prisoners into a room the size of a phone booth. They also had cells where prisoners had to stand for days in three inches of water with no place to sit or lie down. Did you know the arms of straightjackets used to be twelve or fourteen feet long? They'd knot them behind your back.

Late one night Mrs Sabo and I watch a program about a tribe in South America. It shows a naked old guy roasting a yam on a stick. Then it shows a young guy in corduroys riding a moped. The young guy, the narrator lady tells us, is the old guy's grandson. No one wants to do the traditional tribe stuff anymore, the narrator lady says. The old people sit around on their haunches looking gloomy and the youngsters ride buses and move to the cities and listen to cassette tapes. None of the young people want to speak the original language, the narrator lady says, and no one bothers to teach it to their babies. The village used to have 150 people. All but six have moved away and are speaking Spanish now.

At the end the narrator says the tribe's old language has a word for standing in the rain looking at the back of a person you love. She says it has another word for shooting an arrow into an animal poorly, so that it hurts the animal more than is necessary. To call a person this word, in the old language, the lady says, is the worst sort of curse you could imagine.

The River Nemunas

Fog swirls outside the windows. Mrs Sabo stands and disconnects herself from her machine and takes a bottle of Juozo beer from the refrigerator. Then she goes out the front door and walks into the yard and stands at the far edge of the porch light and pours some beer into her cupped hand. She holds it out for a long time, and I'm wondering if Mrs Sabo has finally drifted off the edge until out of the mist comes a white horse and it drinks the beer right out of her cupped hand and then Mrs Sabo presses her forehead against the horse's big face and the two of them stay like that for a long time.

* * *

That night I dream my molars come loose. My mouth fills with teeth. I know before I open my eyes that Mrs Sabo is dead. People come over all day long. Her son leaves the windows and doors open for three days so that her soul can escape. At night I walk over to her house and sit with him. He smokes cigarettes and I watch cooking shows.

The River Nemunas, he says in Lithuanian, two nights after she's gone. He doesn't say anything else.

Two weeks later Grandpa drives me home from school and looks at me a long time and tells me he wants to go fishing.

Really? I say.

Yes, he says. He walks across the field with me; he lets me bait his hook. For three straight afternoons we fish together. He tells me that the chemical plant where Mrs Sabo worked used to make cement and fertilizer and sulfuric acid, and under the Soviets some days the river would turn mustard yellow. He tells me that under the Soviets the farms here were collective farms, where many families worked a large area, and that's why the houses out here are in clusters and not spread out, each to its own plot, like farmhouses in Kansas.

On the fourth day, I'm fishing with a chicken carcass when my line goes tight. I count to three and try to yank my rod up. It doesn't budge. It's a feeling like I've hooked into the river bottom itself, like I'm trying to pull up the bedrock of Lithuania.

Grandpa Z looks over at my line and then at me. Snagged? he says. My arms feel like they're going to tear off. The current pulls the boat slowly downstream and soon the line is so tight drops are sizzling off it. Every once in a while a little line cranks off the reel. That's all that happens. If I were to let go of my rod, it would shoot upriver.

I consider cutting the line. Something pulls at me and the boat pulls at it and we stay like that for a long time, locked in a tug-of-war, my little fishing line holding the entire boat and me and Mishap and Grandpa Z steady

The River Nemunas

against the current, as if I've hooked into a big, impossible plug of sadness resting on the bottom of the river.

You pull, I whisper to myself. Then you crank. Like Mrs Sabo did. Pull, crank, pull, crank.

I try. My arms feel like they're disappearing. The boat rocks. Mishap pants. A bright silver wind comes down the river. It smells like wet pine trees. I close my eyes. I think about Mom's raspberry bushes, Dad's filing cabinet, the new family that's moving into our house, some new Mom hanging her clothes in Mom's closet, some new Dad calling to her from Dad's office, some teenage son tacking posters to my walls. I think about how Grandpa Z says the sky is blue because it's dusty and octopuses can unscrew the tops off jars and starfish have one foot and three mouths. I think: No matter what happens, no matter how wretched and gloomy everything can get, at least Mrs Sabo got to feel this.

Grandpa Z says, It's not a snag. He says it twice. I open my eyes. Bubbles are rising from whatever is on the other end of my line. It's as if I'm going to separate at the waist. But gradually, eventually, I seem to be gaining some ground. The boat rocks as I pull it a yard upstream. I heave the rod up, crank in a couple turns of line.

Pull, then crank. Pull, then crank. We skid another yard upstream. Grandpa Z's little eyes seems about to bulge out of their sockets.

It's not a fish. I know it's not a fish. It's just a big piece of trash at the bottom of the Nemunas River. I say a prayer Dad taught me about God being in the light and the water and the rocks, about God's mercy enduring forever. I say it quickly to myself, hissing it out through my lips, and pull then crank, pull then crank, God is in the light, God is in the water, God is in the rocks, and I can feel Mishap scrabbling around the boat with his little claws and I can even feel his heart beating in his chest, a little bright fist opening and closing, and I can feel the river pulling past the boat, its tributaries like fingernails dragging through the entire country, all of Lithuania draining into this one artery, five hundred sliding miles of water, all the way to the Baltic, which Grandpa Z says is the coldest sea in Europe, and something occurs to me that will probably seem obvious to you but that I never thought about before: a river never stops. Wherever you are, whatever you're doing, forgetting, sleeping, mourning, dying—the rivers are still running.

Grandpa Z shouts. Something is surfacing twenty feet away from the boat. It comes up slowly, like a submarine, as if from a dream: huge, breathtakingly huge, the size of a desk. It's a fish.

I can see four barbells under his snout, like snakes. I see his fog-colored belly. I see the big hook stuck through his jaw. He moves slowly, and eases his head back and forth, like a horse shaking off a wasp.

He is huge. He is tremendous. He is ten feet long.

Erketas, says Grandpa Z.

I can't hold it anymore, I say.

Grandpa Z says, You can.

Pull, crank. Breathe in light, breathe out color. The sturgeon comes to us upside down. His mouth sucks and opens, sucks and opens. His back is covered with armor. He looks fifty thousand years old.

For a full minute the fish floats beside the boat like a soft white railroad tie, the boat rocking gently, no Mrs Sabo, no Mom and Dad, no tape measures or hanging scales, no photographs, my arms ablaze with pain and Mishap barking and Grandpa Z looking down as if he's been asked to witness a resurrection. The sturgeon's gills open and close. The flesh inside the gills is a brilliant, impossible crimson.

I hold him there for maybe ten more seconds. Who else sees him? The cows? The trees? Then Grandpa Z leans over, unfolds his pocketknife, and cuts the line.

The fish floats beside the boat for a few seconds, stunned and sleepy. He doesn't flick his tail, doesn't flex his huge body. He simply sinks out of sight.

Mishap goes quiet. The boat wobbles and starts downriver. The river pours on and on. I think of those photos of Mom, as tall and thin as a blade of grass, a bike rider, a swimmer, a stranger, a suntanned sixth-grader who might still come pedaling up the driveway of her father's house some afternoon with a jump rope over her shoulder. I think of Mrs Sabo, how her memories slipped away one by one into the twilight and left her here in a house in a field in the middle of Lithuania waiting for skinny, ravenous Giltine to carry her to a garden on the other side of the sky.

I feel the tiniest lightening. Like one pound out of a thousand has been lifted off my shoulders. Grandpa Z slowly dips his hands in the water and rubs them together. I can see each drop of water falling off his fingertips. I can see them dropping in perfect spheres and merging with the river.

* * *

We hardly ever talk about the fish. It's there between us, something we share. Maybe we believe talking about it will ruin it. Grandpa Z spends his evenings etching Mrs Sabo's face into her tombstone. Her son has offered several times to pay but Grandpa does it for free. He puts her on the granite without her glasses and her eyes look small and naked and girlish. He draws a lace-collared dress up tight around her throat and pearls around that, and he renders her hair in cotton-candy loops. It really is a very good job. It rains on the day they put it over her grave.

In November our whole school takes a bus to Plokštinė, an abandoned underground Soviet missile base where the Russians used to keep nukes. It looks like a grassy field, hemmed with birch, with an oversized pitcher's mound in each corner. There are no admission fees, no tourists, just a few signs in English and Lithuanian and a single strand of barbed wire—all that remains of seven layers of alarms, electric fences, razor cable, Dobermans, searchlights, and machine gun emplacements.

We go down a staircase in the center of the field. Electric bulbs dangle from cracked ceilings. The walls are cramped and rusty. I pass a tiny bunk room and a pair of generators with their guts torn out. Then a dripping black corridor, clotted with puddles. Eventually I reach a railing. The ceiling is belled out: one of the pitcher's mounds must be directly above me. I shine my flashlight ninety feet down. The bottom of the silo is all rust and shadows and echoes.

Here, not so long ago, they kept a thermonuclear ballistic missile as big as a tractor trailer. The iron collar around the rim of the hole has the 360 degrees of a compass painted around its circumference. Easier, I suppose, to aim for a compass heading than for Frankfurt.

The urge to know scrapes against the inability to know. What was Mrs Sabo's life like? What was my mother's? We peer at the past through murky water; all we can see are shapes and figures. How much is real? And how much is merely threads and tombstones?

On the way home Lithuanian kids jostle in the seats around me, smelling of body odour. A stork flaps across a field in the last of the daylight. The boy beside me tells me to keep my eyes out the window, that to see a white horse at dusk is the best possible kind of luck.

* * *

Don't tell me how to grieve. Don't tell me ghosts fade away eventually, like they do in movies, waving goodbye with see-through hands. Lots of things fade away but ghosts like these don't. Heartbreak like this doesn't. The axe blade is still as sharp and real inside me as it was six months ago.

I do my homework and feed my dog and say my prayers. Grandpa Z learns a little more English, I learn a little more Lithuanian, and soon both of us can talk in the past tense. And when I start to feel the Big Sadness cutting me up inside I try to remember Mrs Sabo and the garden that is the afterworld and I watch the birds fly south in their flocks.

The River Nemunas

The sturgeon we caught was pale and armored and beautiful, splotched all over with age and lice. He was a big soft-boned hermit living at the bottom of a deep hole in a river that pours on and on like a green ghost through the fields of Lithuania. Is he an orphan like me? Does he spend all day every day searching for someone else he recognizes? And yet, wasn't he so gentle when I got him close to the boat? Wasn't he just as patient as a horse? Wasn't he just about as noble as anything?

Jesus, Dad used to say, is a golden boat on a long, dark river. That's one thing I can remember him saying.

It's quiet in Lithuania in November, and awful dark. I lie on my grandfather's bed and clutch Mishap and breathe in light and breathe out colour. The house groans. I pray for Mom and Dad and Mrs Sabo and Grandpa Z. I pray for those South American tribespeople on the television and their vanishing language. I pray for the lonely sturgeon, a monster, a lunker, last elder of a dying nation, drowsing in the bluest, deepest chambers of the River Nemunas.

Out the window it starts to snow.

The Intrepid Dumpling's Dugong Story

by Louisa Young

One day the Intrepid Dumpling turned up at the court of the Troll Queen. They were lying on her sofa after dinner and the Troll Queen said, 'Tell me a story'.

'What about?' asked the Intrepid Dumpling.

'A dugong,' said the Troll Queen.

'Once upon a time,' said the Intrepid Dumpling, 'a beautiful young dugong was strolling through the forest, flapping her floppy feet and bending her skinny knees, so her fluffy round body rose and fell among the ferns the way dugongs do...'

'Hold on a minute,' said the Troll Queen. 'You don't know what a dugong is, do you?'

'I didn't think they *were*,' confessed the Intrepid Dumpling. 'I thought you wanted me to invent one.'

'A dugong is a sea cow,' said the Troll Queen. 'It's like a giant seal, or very beautiful sea lion. In the Olden Days sailors used to mistake them for mermaids.'

'I thought it would be like an ostrich,' said the Intrepid Dumpling.

'Well it's not,' said the Troll Queen. 'Go on.'

The Intrepid Dumpling started again, and this is the story she told:

Once upon a time, a beautiful young dugong and

The Intrepid Dumpling's Dugong Story

her old, old grandmother were splashing along the beach, dipping their noses in the rockpools, looking for oysters to do business with. The reason they were doing it was this: the King of the Dugongs had a son, who was absolutely horrible. He was as slimy and grimy and horrible as our dugong was sleek and golden and sprightly. He had atrocious manners and only ever thought about himself (our dugong, on the other hand, was kind and courteous, and particularly good to her old Grandma).

Well, the King of the Dugongs wanted his son to get married, and he wanted him to marry someone wonderful, because that way, he said, he had a chance of getting some halfway decent grandchildren. And he wanted him to marry soon because the sooner the halfway decent grandchildren were born, the sooner they would be old enough to take over from their horrible father, and save the Dugong Kingdom from a terrible ruler.

So the King of the Dugongs rang up all his friends on his beautiful long curly shell telephone and asked them who was the best and nicest and cleverest young dugong girl in the kingdom.

The first three girls who were suggested were indeed very good and nice. They were thoughtful and clean and intelligent and one even had a sense of humour. But they were also rich, and their kind thoughtful intelligent rich parents were so upset at the prospect of their daughters marrying the bilious scurrilous prince that they each took the Dugong King aside in turn and had a word in his lustrous furry ear. As each of them whispered in turn, the King's face went from hopeful to sad to hopeful to ashamed to resigned. Each of the parents gave the King a large cheque and, because the Dugong Prince's extravagant gambling habit and taste for expensive foreign ice-creams had almost bankrupted the Dugong Kingdom, the King shamefacedly accepted the money and let the nice young dugong girls go home to their fond families and relieved boyfriends.

And this is where our dugong comes in - because our dugong was the fourth best and nicest dugong girl in all the kingdom (according to some. Others felt she was nicer than that). And our dugong had one quality that the other three had lacked - she was penniless. Her old grandmother couldn't afford a large cheque, and that is why, on that cloudy day, the two of them were splashing along the beach, trying to persuade the oysters to part with their pearls. They hoped they might collect something to offer the King in place of our dugong's flipper in marriage.

They weren't doing very well. And their hearts weren't really in it, because they knew that the oysters needed their pearls for a rainy day. Even though they

The Intrepid Dumpling's Dugong Story

could grow new ones, few of them could afford to give up their nest eggs. So our dugong and her Grandma had only collected three pearls when a palace guard appeared, saying 'Tssccchh! We've been looking for you everywhere. You have to come to the palace, right now.' And then our dugong gave even those three pearls away, to a tattered family of little sea squirts who had lost their mother, sitting by the side of the road leading to the King of the Dugongs' strange and beautiful underwater palace.

'Whatever shall we do?' whispered Grandma, as they were ushered in to the King of the Dugongs' palatial audience chamber. It was lined with conch shells as pink and shiny as the curlicues down on our dugong's pretty ears, and illuminated by thousands of iridescent squid, whose luminous multi-coloured tentacles dangled from the murky, cavernous depths of the ceiling. Beneath them hovered tiny gleaming jellyfish, red and gold and green, whose job was to dash to the side of anybody who didn't have enough light to read by.

'Oh Lawdy,' said Grandma, looking up through the crowd of shining courtiers to the dais where the King sat resplendent on a huge plush sea cucumber. 'Oh Lawdy.' For beside the King, sprawled across a smaller cucumber, covered in gungey barnacles, whiskers dripping with slime, eyes dull and shifty, snout curled in a sneer and flippers stained yellow from smoking, lounged the Dugong Prince. Even his nasty ears were limp and unfriendly.

'Oh Lawdy Lawdy,' said Grandma. 'Oh Lawdy Lawdy Lawdy.' But our dugong just looked at the horrible prince, shook her pretty golden head, blinked her dark golden eyes, and set to thinking.

Then the King stood up, and coughed, and addressed them. 'Um... excuse me!' he said. 'Could you come over here?'

Our dugong and Grandma slithered between the courtiers (silver and crimson) up to the front of the dais, and looked up at the king. No-one else was taking any notice of him at all; they were all too busy flapping their flippers and wiggling their fins and wrinkling up their snouts. But then the King coughed again, very loudly, and said: 'Oy, you lot, straighten up, would you?' And all the courtiers sprang to attention in elegant and impressive rows against the pink curly walls.

'Now,' said the Dugong King.

'Oh no,' whispered Grandma.

'Ahhh,' sighed the courtiers.

'Well actually,' said our dugong, 'it's all right.'

'Is it?' said the King, in surprise. 'I'm sure it's not. You see, I want you to... I'm so sorry, my dear, but I want you to marry him. He's just got to have decent children, you

The Intrepid Dumpling's Dugong Story

see, or just imagine what everyone will have to put up with when he's king...'

The Dugong Prince was picking his snout, ignoring everyone.

'And you see,' continued the King, 'You're the best and nicest girl in the kingdom who's not rich enough to get out of it. You even gave those seasquirts the three pearls which were your only hope of escape from marrying that...' and the King gestured towards his son, who was rolling up a big bogey between his flippers.

'But it's all right,' said our dugong.

The Prince opened up his mouth to pop the bogey in.

'I've already decided to marry him.'

The Prince's mouth opened wide with astonishment.

'I'll marry him happily,' she said. 'Someone has to, and it might as well be me, if you want me. I'll be glad to marry him.'

At that the Prince opened his mouth so wide that the top of his horrible head began to fall back, and back, and back. And suddenly it fell off entirely, and the ever-widening astonished mouth split the slimy green barnacled head right in half. And then out of the scummy green throat came a cry—and suddenly the whole limp, splodgy, scurfy body fell in two, and from it leapt a handsome young dugong as sleek and dark and golden and sprightly as our own, with perky whiskers and a dashing look in his eye.

'Dad!' he cried. 'I'm so sorry! Do you remember when I ran off when I was four? I stole some of Neptune's apples and he cursed me with horribleness so no-one would marry me. He said that only someone volunteering to marry me of their own accord would break the spell! Nasty, eh? But you—' and here he turned to our dugong, clasped her to his sleek bosom and gazed into her golden eyes '—you have saved me and the Kingdom from a horrible fate.' And on the spot he presented her with a crown of trained seahorses, who would swim in circles above her golden brow, and a pair of beautiful seahorse earrings, who would swim forever just beneath her pretty ears, and every now and then wiggle up to whisper jokes into them, for seahorses are famous for their sense of humour.

The Intrepid Dumpling leaned back on the sofa and looked at the Troll Queen expectantly. The Troll Queen looked back.

'Then what happened?' she asked.

'They got married and lived happily ever after, of course,' said the Intrepid Dumpling. 'Don't you know anything about stories?'

'Well you didn't say so,' said the Troll Queen.

'Well they did,' said the Intrepid Dumpling.

The Intrepid Dumpling's Dugong Story

'I thought it might be different this time,' said the Troll Queen.

'Oh no,' said the Dugong. 'It's just the same. That's one of the nicest things about stories.'

The Loris

by Romesh Gunesekera

How The Loris Learnt What To Do

My name is Lorrie and I usually like to take things easy. I am a very slow slender loris.

I live in a tree with my mother. My tree is tall and I have a spot of my own about fifty feet up from the ground. I can see right across the pond to the mango trees on the other side. From the first time I saw the fruit, I wanted to go over and eat one. But my mother had said, 'Don't bother. By the time you get there, the mangoes would have fallen. The season would be over.'

I didn't believe her. I could see the mangoes grow bigger, turn from green to yellow and ripen ever so slowly. Green parrots flew in and pecked at them. The fruit didn't fall for ages. I told my mother, 'Look, they are still there.'

Her large unblinking eyes softened. 'It is a long way to go around the water. It will take you many, many nights. You will have to avoid the grassland on the left and stick to the trees. You will have to go so far in, you will lose sight of the water. The moon will vanish. You might get lost in enemy territory. There are many predators: leopards, pythons, dragons. But even if you don't get lost, by the time you get to the mangoes, the fruit will be rotten. We are slow movers.'

I don't know why she didn't even want me to try.

* * *

The rains came. There was thunder in the sky. In the north and the south, big animals waged war. We slept. I like to sleep. I like to dream. Sometimes even when my eyes are open, I am dreaming. My favourite dream is about mangoes. Green mangoes slowly turning yellow like the sun. In my dream I eat the sun. I feel warm inside and everything becomes night. Then, in my dream, I move like a dream. Fast as light falling at dusk.

* * *

Last week, I saw them again. Small, round, green bobbles on the trees across the pond appeared like a starburst in a faraway galaxy. Each one destined to turn into a sun, in the shape of a teardrop. An island. A day later nothing much had changed. I remembered what had happened last season and reckoned I had quite a few nights to get over to the mangoes. I couldn't disappear for that long without telling my mother, so I told her.

'It is too dangerous,' she said. 'Please, don't go.'

'Don't worry,' I said. 'You will be able to see me most

of the time. It is only between the coconut trees that I will be out of sight. I'll bring you back a mango.'

'I don't want a mango,' she said. 'I want you to be safe here.'

'Don't you want me to do what I dream of doing?'

'I do.'

'Then, let me go,' I said and hugged her.

* * *

It took me three nights to get to the water's edge and another three to get to the breadfruit tree that stretched over the stream. Progress was slow because I had to test each branch I used. Some were weak and would bend for the weight of a swallow. Others were short and I could not easily reach a connecting one. Sometimes I had to retrace my steps. But there was never any danger. I heard no other animals in the trees, up where I climbed. The monkeys were too heavy for my branches, even the tree squirrels couldn't get close. Although I once heard a leopard coughing at the water, it did not frighten me. He would have had no way of reaching me and even when my branches dipped we were still way up in the safe canopy of the jungle. The difficulty was the breadfruit tree. The branch that bridged the stream was as big as an elephant's leg. Anything could walk on

The Loris

it. It would take me from dusk to dawn to get across as my top speed is only about three feet an hour and I can keep that up only for a couple of hours at a time. If an enemy came while I was crossing, I would be in trouble. Big trouble.

I spent the afternoon watching the heron fishing in the pond. He is always on his own, stooped and morose. When he catches a fish he shows no mercy, gobbling it up straightaway. Sometimes he raises his grey wings like an avatar, but he has nothing to offer us. I like it when the fish jump just out of his reach and make ripples in the purple water like anger in his mind. Then he becomes a little dizzy and wobbles.

As the sun sank behind the trees, and the bats started to launch out into the black sky, one after another, I inched down towards the lower branches of the big tree. The biggest branch, when I reached it, was knotted and spongy. It was peculiarly furry and prickled my hands and feet. I felt it move in the slow rhythm of a sleeper's breath. It dawned on me that I was walking across a leopard's back. When I reached its ear, the leopard woke up. I quickly slid down a few inches. The leopard slowly stretched and stood up but did not notice me. I am very light. Then, to my amazement, he crept along the branch, ferrying me to the other side. On the ground he moved swiftly and took me all the way to the mango trees. What a thrill to move at such speed!

When I saw my dream fruit, I grabbed a passing cane and parted company. The leopard rushed into the undergrowth and vanished.

I had learnt my most important lesson: what you can't do by yourself, you might be able to do with the help of someone else.

By the time I reached the branches where the fruit hung like coloured drops, a few had begun to ripen. I found one that a red-beaked parrot had ripped open. Inside the skin, in the golden soft fruit, I discovered heaven. I had never tasted anything so delicious. I ate and ate and ate, high up in the trees, safe and sweet. I ate all afternoon and all night. My dream had come true. I felt I was eating the sun.

Then, in the early morning, when the light was struggling to wake, to break out of the clouds, the sky seemed to get very angry with me. A howling and shrieking filled the air. Piercing screams. A huge metal bird burst out of the clouds and swooped down. The breadfruit tree exploded. The thunder was deafening. More explosions followed, one after the other, and the heat of several suns colliding singed the trees around me. A moment later, an enormous fire blazed and tree after tree ignited. The fire rushed towards me. I was petrified. Some humans appeared with guns. They fired at the

The Loris

sky. Another metal bird screamed down with its fiery droppings. More explosions. Mangoes fell to the ground. Branches. Trees. Birds. Monkeys.

I said goodbye to my mother, in my heart. I was sorry. Perhaps I should have heeded her. But I was not sorry to have tasted the mango. Even if our world was destroyed, at least I had tasted heaven. Was that bad? Should I not have done it? Was this onslaught somehow my fault?

I shifted a few inches down the branch. The fire was moving as fast as my thoughts, speeding over the ground, crackling twigs and grass and bushes. Animals I had never seen so close before broke out of the bush just ahead of the flames: pigs, iguanas, wild cats and deer. Then my leopard appeared. A human saw it and fired a shot. The leopard growled. The man dropped his gun and fled. The leopard leapt over the flames and came towards the mango trees. He stopped under my tree and looked back over his shoulder. My steps may be slow, but in my head I can think as fast as anyone.

I let go.

I landed on his neck, where I had been perched before. The heat of the blaze cracked trees and broke branches. He did not notice me with all the debris falling around. More humans appeared, shouting. The leopard with me on his back slipped into the water. I crawled to the top of his head, fast enough to get there as his body submerged and I sailed across the pond homeward.

When we finally reached the other side of the pond, the leopard padded up under the trees and shook himself, sending me flying up with the water drops. I caught the branch of my old tree. I was home and dry.

In our world even our enemies can become our friends. I wished the humans could too.

* * *

I found my mother just before dusk. She was waiting for me. We watched the flames rise and fall on the far side of the pond and I told her what the sun tasted like, and what it felt like to rush at speed, to sail across water, to fly in the air.

Her face turned slowly from side to side. 'But how did you do it?'

I told her we can do what we dream of, despite the fires of war, by remembering what we learn and learning not to fear. I said, 'You can move as fast as you wish, if you follow your heart but also use your head.'

APPENDIX

Bears

Deforestation and expansion of land used for agriculture have seriously impacted upon bear habitats. Bears are hunted legally for recreation. They are also poached for their skins as rugs and trophies. Body parts from bears are used to supply the traditional Chinese medicine trade and exotic meat market.

Their fat, skin, paws, bones, claws, gall bladders and bile are used for traditional medicines, meals in expensive restaurants or as charms.

Chimpanzee

Deforestation is driving chimpanzees toward extinction. As forests are cleared for living space, growing crops and grazing for domestic livestock, the chimps who live there disappear. Forest concessions are sold to timber companies from the developed world, some of which practice clear cutting, turning forest habitats into desert.

As logging roads are cut into previously unreachable areas, the hunting of wildlife for bushmeat—once a practice supporting forest peoples—has become commercial, catering to the tastes of urban dwellers for the "exotic" meats of wild animals.

The Dugong

Dugongs are believed to have been the basis of mermaid legends. They have been hunted for thousands of years for their meat and oil. Today the Convention on International Trade in Endangered Species (CITES) limits, or bans, the trade of derived products. Despite being legally protected in many countries the main causes of population decrease include hunting, habitat degradation, and fishing-related fatalities. With its long lifespan of 70 years or more, and slow rate of reproduction, the dugong is especially vulnerable to these types of exploitation.

The Chiru Antelope

The Chiru is killed for its soft fleecy underwool known as shahtoosh, which is made into shawls. One of the most expensive materials in the world, worth its weight in gold several times over, shatoosh means "king of wools" in Persian.

Shahtoosh shawls can sell in the United States for up to $30,000. It takes the fur of three to five chiru to make one six-foot shawl.

A global ban on shahtoosh sales was introduced in 2002. Shahtoosh is still in high demand and smuggling operations meet that demand. In many countries shahtoosh shawls are sold by wealthy women who operate like drug dealers.

The Coppersmith Barbet

A bird with a crimson forehead and throat which is best known for its metronomic call that has been likened to a coppersmith striking metal with a hammer. It is a resident found in South Asia and parts of Southeast Asia. Like other barbets, they chisel out a hole inside a tree to build their nest. They are mainly fruit-eating but will sometimes take insects, especially winged termites.

Elephants

African elephant numbers, between 1970 and 1989, fell from 1,200,000 to 600,000 as a result of the trade in ivory. Ivory is used for jewellery, carvings and hankos (name stamps carrying the personal seal of the owner). There are fewer than 50,000 Asian elephants left in the world.

The Pinta Island Tortoise

The tortoises of the Galápagos Islands were hunted for their meat by sailors and fishermen to the point of extinction. In addition their habitat was destroyed by the introduction of goats from the mainland. Lonesome George is the last known Pinta Island tortoise, an international icon for conservation efforts. George lives at the Charles Darwin Research Station in the Galápagos Islands.

The Irrawaddy Dolphin

The Irrawaddy dolphins of Myanmar's Ayerwaddy river have been helping fishermen with their catch for centuries. They and Asia's river dolphins are some of the world's most critically endangered species. In 2006, the Baji or Yangtze River dolphin was declared functionally extinct—the first Cetacean species to be driven to extinction, and in our century.

Lady Birds

Ironically Hanif Kureshi's celebration of the musical ladybirds is a poignant reminder of a could-be threatened species.
A new ladybird has recently arrived in Great Britain. But not just any ladybird: this is the harlequin ladybird, the most invasive ladybird on Earth.
The harlequin ladybird was introduced to North America in 1988, where it is now the most widespread ladybird species on the continent. It has already invaded much of north-western Europe,

and arrived in Britain in summer 2004.

There are 46 species of ladybird resident in Britain and the recent arrival of the harlequin ladybird has the potential to jeopardise many of these.

The Leatherback Turtle

The Leatherback turtle faces threats on both nesting beaches and in the marine environment. The greatest causes of decline and the continuing primary threats to leatherbacks worldwide are long-term harvest and incidental capture in commercial fisheries. The harvest of eggs and adults occurs on nesting beaches where juveniles and adults are harvested. Marine pollution (such as balloons and plastic bags floating in the water, which are mistaken for jellyfish) is an added threat. Together these threats are serious ongoing sources of mortality that adversely affect the species' recovery.

The Pink Headed Duck

The last sighting of a pink-headed duck was in 1949. This large diving duck, was once found in parts of the Gangetic Plains of India, Bangladesh and in the riverine swamps of Myanmar, could possibly be extinct.

This elusive bird is extremely hard to find as it is difficult to reach their natural habitat to see them. They are also shy timid birds. They could possibly exist in the inaccessible swamp regions of northern Myanmar and some sighting reports from that region have led to its status being declared as "critically endangered" rather than extinct.

The Sarus Crane

The Sarus Crane is the only resident breeding crane in India and

Southeast Asia, and is the world's tallest flying bird. The future of the Indian Sarus Crane is closely tied to the quality of small wetlands in India that experience heavy human use. Destruction of wetlands due to agricultural expansion is increasing dramatically and poses a significant threat throughout the range of Sarus Cranes. In India, mortality due to collision with electrical wires is a significant threat and cranes have died due to pesticide poisoning.

Seahorses

The use of seahorses for traditional Chinese medicine takes the lives of about 20 million sea horses per year. Although seahorses are popular for their medicinal value and are claimed to be effective treatments, no research has been done to prove if they are. Seahorses are also popular souvenirs dried and attached to key rings. Never buy products made from seahorses.

Sea Turtles

Many countries still allow the commercial exploitation of sea turtles for food, oil, leather, and jewellery. Turtle skin can be turned into leather and is used for shoes and handbags, while its shell is used to make sunglasses, trinkets and jewellery. Sometimes the entire carcass is stuffed and sold as a souvenir or turned into novelty items such as musical instruments. Never buy products made from tortoiseshell.

The Silky Sifaka

The local people of Madagascar say that Silkies "fly like angels", leaping as far as ten yards from tree to tree. A large lemur characterized by long, silky white fur. Living in a much restricted range in North Eastern Madagascar, the Silky Sifaka is one of the rarest mammals on earth. Illegal logging of precious wood, such as rosewood and ebony which continues even within protected rainforests areas is a major threat to the survival of the remaining population which numbers less than 1000. Time is quickly running out for the Silky Safaka.

The Slow Loris

This endearing creature has become a victim of the pet trade. A popular pet in Japan, a slow loris will cost you between $1,500 and $4,500. These creatures are not suitable as pets and can endure great cruelty.

Despite a ban in domestic trade in the slow loris, trade is widespread and carried out in an open manner.

International trade in the slow loris is also banned by the Convention on International Trade in Endangered Species (CITES).

Sturgeon

Several species of sturgeon are considered threatened with extinction as a result of over-fishing, poaching, water pollution, damming and destruction of natural watercourses and habitats.

Sturgeon fishing and trade in the products is a very profitable business. Compared to other fishery activities it is often viewed as "gold-mining". Illegal harvest and trade in sturgeon products is a well managed and operated business, controlled by organised crime and associated with world-wide corruption. Over-fishing and poaching has led to a significant reduction in total legal catch in the world and especially in the main sturgeon basin—the Caspian Sea.

The Tasmanian Tiger

A striped marsupial the size of a dog, the last captive "thylacine" died in a Tasmanian zoo in 1936. The most recently found remains have been dated as being about 2,200 years old. The arrival of European settlers in Tanzania marked the end for the Tasmanian Tiger. Excessive hunting combined with habitat destruction are believed to have been the main cause for their extinction.

There have been hundreds of alleged sightings of Tasmanian Tigers since 1936 but all these sightings have remained inconclusive. Web sites are devoted to the search for the tiger but it is unlikely to still exist.

The Tiger

Tigers are being hunted into extinction for their skin, bone and penis. Tiger bone is used in traditional Asian medicine to treat ailments such as rheumatism, joint and back pain, paralysis and leprosy.

In Asia, the bones of a single poached tiger can fetch up to US$30,000. Tiger penis is believed to treat impotency and demands high prices as an "exotic" food, a bowl of tiger penis soup costing up to US$320 in Taiwan. The tiger's skin is also highly coveted on the luxury market for rugs and other decoration.